MIDNIGHT MOON

It was truly a night made for lovers, Zevia thought, not mere acquaintances like her and Sam. The welcoming salt spray of the ocean cooled her flushed face as reluctantly she allowed herself to stand beside Sam on the upper deck.

The ocean was a sea of black, but the *Eastern Queen* clipped easily over white, frothy, breaking waves. The moon, splendidly bright, was beautiful as it rode through the black velvet sky. Brilliant diamond-like stars studded the heavens.

Sam was tall, with bronze sun-burnished skin and his eyes were dark, a deep brown that seemed to Zevia to be able to penetrate the heavens. She could tell by his enthusiasm that he was eager to share his knowledge of sea and sky with her.

"See, Miss Sinclair, there's the Southern Cross, a constellation found only in the southern hemisphere."

"It's beautiful," Zevia breathed as she tried to ingnore the flush within her own body caused by Sam's nearness. She could feel his warm breath against her ear as he continued to tell her how important this constellation was to sailors.

My own body is turning against me, Zevia exclaimed to herself. *What's wrong with me?*

MIDNIGHT MOON

MILDRED RILEY

PINNACLE BOOKS
KENSINGTON PUBLISHING CORP.

PINNACLE BOOKS are published by

Kensington Publishing Corp.
850 Third Avenue
New York, NY 10022

The Arabesque logo Reg. U.S. Pat. & TM Off. Arabesque is
a trademark of Kensington Publishing Corp.

First Printing: November, 1995

Printed in the United States of America

Acknowledgments

The author wishes to acknowledge the invaluable assistance of the following institutions: the Peabody Museum of Salem, Massachusetts; the Peter Foulger Museum/Research Center, Nantucket, Massachusetts; the USS *Constitution* Museum of Boston, Massachusetts; and the South Street Seaport Museum in New York City, New York.

M. E. R.
March 10, 1995
Whitman, Massachusetts

Prologue

Zevia's agonizing screams went unheard during the height of the tumultuous storm. Dorcas and her husband, Josiah, the ship's cook, busily preparing hot coffee and warm grog for the weary men who stumbled below deck, heard nothing except the howling wind and the beating rain on the deck below.

It was nearly three in the morning before the harsh elements subsided, and it was only then that Dorcas remembered her promise to check on the ailing girl.

She placed a hot toddy and some crackers on a tray, and tapped lightly on the cabin door.

Weak, feeble moans came from behind it. Quickly, Dorcas pushed it open.

"What's wrong, child?" Her eyes widened at what she saw.

"Where all this blood come from?"

Dorcas heard only a breathless whimper.

"My . . . my monthly flow! Dorcas, I have such pain! Help me, please help me."

Zevia's voice trailed into a whimper and Dorcas sprang into action. A swift examination of the blood, the clots, the drained pallor of Zevia's face told her what had happened.

There was distinct sorrow in her face when she spoke. "Child, ain't no monthly. You done lost a baby."

Zevia stared at Dorcas as the words penetrated her brain. What she had feared had happened.

At least Papa and Oma will never know, she thought. Tears welled in her eyes.

Ashamed, she turned her face away from Dorcas, who with the wisdom of generations knew that Zevia had chosen to face her travail alone.

Instinctively, Dorcas held Zevia close. The gesture seemed to release the tension within Zevia's tight frame and she sobbed openly.

"My momma died when I was born, and I was so scared . . . didn't know . . ." she wailed tearfully.

"Sh, sh, it's all right. Honey, everything's going to be all right. God has a way of helpin' us with our mistakes," she said.

She pushed aside the sodden sheets, grabbed a towel, and pressed it firmly between Zevia's trembling legs. Gently, she bathed the girl's face and arms, and then she helped her into a clean nightgown.

"Here," she said, "you need this."

She helped Zevia drink the warm, stimulating liquid and eat a cracker. Then she put Zevia's feet up on a pillow and tucked an extra blanket around the girl's shaking body before she turned to leave.

At the cabin door, she said, "Stay real quiet and get some sleep. I'll check on you soon. She gathered up the bloody evidence and started to leave. Her sympathy for the unhappy girl was evident when she spoke from the open doorway.

"Miss Zevia, it's over now. Over and done with. Just one of the many hardships in this here life, being a woman. But you be strong. I know you can do that. Saw it in your face. Don't look back! Ever! Another thing," she said quietly, "you ain't the first somebody who's been tricked—you won't be the last!"

Dorcas closed the door gently behind her, the visible proof of Zevia's transgression tucked under her arm. There was plenty of blood and gore from the accidents of the men who had been battling the storm; no one would notice a few more bloody sheets. She shook her head when she recalled Zevia's troubled face. Ever since Eve, women have been tricked, she thought. Some bastard took advantage of the girl, she'd bet on that—poor motherless child.

Dorcas was so deep in her thoughts, she did not see the man standing transfixed in the dark shadows near Zevia's cabin.

Part One

One

Germany, 1805

Alexander Sinclair closed the heavy oak door quietly behind him. Frau Erlans appeared out of the dark recesses of the corridor to help him remove his loden greatcoat. It was heavily sprinkled with snow, and she shook it vigorously before hanging it on the clothes tree.

"Come, come at once to the master's room. All day he calls for you," she whispered. "I asked should I send for his sister, Frau Fleishman, and her son, his nephew, but he said, *'Nein,* only you he wants.' "

In the darkened room, heavy brocade draperies had been drawn over the narrow floor-to-ceiling windows. A fire in the stone fireplace murmured as soft burned chunks of ash fell from the andirons. The only other light in the room flickered feebly from an old, elaborate candelabrum on the bedside table.

Alex thought he would choke; there seemed to be no air in the dying man's room. It was so stifling, Alex could scarcely breathe. His father lay on a thick bank of pillows, propped high to ease his labored breathing. The respiratory sounds alternated from wet, bubbling noises to hissing wheezes as thin air escaped his lungs. He was covered with comforters and quilts as if they could keep the cold fingers of death from reaching him.

"Father?" Alex questioned hesitantly, as he neared the bed.

"Alex, my son, come, come." The hoarse whispers sounded strange to Alex's ears. Where was the booming voice that had always issued authoritative commands to him? The sounds he heard now from the desiccated shell of a man were like those of a wounded, trapped animal.

Noxious odors came from beneath the covers as the man's hand reached to grasp Alex's.

"Forgive me, son . . . I did not mean . . . to hurt you. I wanted . . . wanted so much for you to have more." His voice almost failed. Then, with great effort, he struggled to continue. "More, I thought, than . . . than they could give you."

The physical effort and the emotional impact of those few words were almost more than the man could afford in his dying state. His energy was almost spent. He seemed to require an extraordinary effort to continue speaking. He rested for a brief moment, as if trying to summon his failing vitality. His bony hand retreated again under the bedcovers. He thrust a small brass key into Alex's hand.

"All you need . . . bottom of the chest." He turned his wizened, frail head toward the heavy wooden bureau on the far wall.

"Forgive me," he wheezed, as a bubbly gurgle slipped through his pale blue lips. It was the last sound he made. Soundlessly, his head fell back against the pillows. The old mercenary, Prussian soldier of fortune, volunteer in the British Army, who had fought against the revolutionaries, was dead. Not on the battlefield, as he would have preferred, but in a small, bleak house on a narrow street in a German city, to be mourned ever so slightly by his housekeeper, Frau Erlans, and his adopted son, Alexander Sinclair.

Alex looked at the ocean. The clean salt spray sprinkled him with a freshness he found pleasing to his open face, like a light touch of baptismal dew. Indeed, he felt brand new, a newborn, a fledgling about to leave the nest.

The old soldier, his father, had written "Stoningham, Maine" on his papers. The information found in the locked drawer told Alex what had been kept from him for eighteen years. A child of color, at four, he had been sent as an indentured servant to Herr Tiedemann by his parents. The Hessian had taken him to Germany, promising the boy's parents a better life for their son than he could have had in the hardscrabble state of Maine. As he looked out over the water, Alex Sinclair wondered, would his folks remember their four-year-old? For him, there were only shadowy memories of a tearful goodbye. He remembered little else.

The British barque *Emmaline* sailed placidly in a steady, rhythmic motion as her bow rode the waves. The sensation was pleasant, Alex thought. A voice broke into his thoughts.

"And the top o' the mornin' to ye, sir!"

With a snap of his heels, Alex turned sharply to respond to the voice behind him. He bowed in a formal manner as he recognized the speaker as a ship's officer.

"Güten Tag, mien Herr," he stammered. "I mean, good morning, sir!"

The first mate had noticed the slender young Negro when he had first come aboard the previous day. After almost thirty years at sea, Andrew Larkin had seen much, he thought, but a young black, finely dressed and groomed and with a military bearing, was a far cry from the rough black seamen, ex-slaves, and stevedores he usually encountered.

"Sailin' to America, are ye?"

"Yes, sir. On my way home, sir."

The first mate recognized that this young man was a different kind of Negro. This one looked him in the eye as an equal, did not have his head lowered in a submissive manner, and first mate Andrew Larkin found himself accepting a firm handshake from the brown hand that had been offered. There was an immediate rapport between the two men. Larkin listened with interest and respect as Alex continued.

"I am returning to Maine. I have been away since I was four."

"And now?"

"Now I am twenty-two. Eighteen years I have been away from home."

"Well, 'tis a fine time to come back. Good changes are happening, now that the colonists have declared their independence from Great Britain."

Alex stared at the rolling waves for a moment before he answered, as if trying to control the sudden surge of emotion that overcame him—a feeling of fresh hope that he desperately wanted.

"I hope you are correct, sir."

Larkin noted the slight German accent and the clipped, precise manner with which the young man spoke.

"I expect to find work and make my way in the New

World," Alex offered, and by way of explanation, added, "I was apprenticed to a draftsman."

"Ah, a noble occupation," the first mate agreed. "Have ye ever thought o' designing a ship?" he asked.

He focused on the young man's face.

"I could try," was the prompt answer.

"We need new ships of a speedy shape to make good money," Larkin said.

Larkin took a closer look at the smooth brown skin and noticed the jet black eyes that returned his examining look with straightforward, unflinching eye contact.

Larkin prided himself on his judgment of men. He had worked long enough at sea to have met all types of men. Some had a history of piracy, some were on the sea for selfish reasons—to make money in any way imaginable. Some fled the arm of the law, some the arms of clutching, whining women. He'd seen them all. Men of many races, religious beliefs, and uncertain occupations (honorable and otherwise), but somehow, this young man was different. What had made him so?

When Adelaide Summers saw Alex Sinclair stride up from the beach, she recognized him as a stranger. She watched entranced. Here was a man of color, a rarity on the Maine coast. She noticed the strength of his stride as his long legs brought him closer to her secluded spot.

The late-afternoon sun glowed on his bronze skin, giving it a warm, smooth patina. The planes of his face were strongly etched by the sun's rays. He looked like a golden god, someone from an old history book. Adelaide saw, too, the firm purpose to the set of his mouth. Here is a man who knows how to go after what he wants, she thought.

As she watched from her unseen vantage position, she noticed that with his head thrust forward, he moved with easy grace on the heavily pebbled beach. His dark great-coat billowed behind him like a mainsail. The rhythmic way he moved his arms as he walked intrigued Adelaide. His steps brought him closer to her. The greatcoat opened as he moved, and she could see his broad chest, slender waist, and firm thighs. She held her breath. The grayish-green high-crowned hat he wore made her think of some-one out of a fairy tale.

Nestled in the gray rocks that lined the beach between sea and land, Adelaide pulled her shawl closer around her shoulders. She often sat on the rocks that had been warmed by the spring sun and watched the Atlantic Ocean as it surged in and out along the rocky Maine coastline. Sometimes she'd take lunch with her, and sometimes she'd have a book to read as she sat. But mostly she watched the waves and daydreamed about faraway places and people.

She watched the intriguing stranger move intently along the rocky beach until he finally disappeared be-yond the cove toward the village. Adelaide thought to herself, he must be a free man, dressed the way he is in those fine clothes. Oh, well, another exciting mystery from the sea. Someday she'd move past these rocky shoals and sail on the vast ocean to distant shores to see more of the world than Stoningham, Maine. But, she sighed to herself, for now, Blossom, their cow, was wait-ing, and if she didn't want to hear her mother's frequent instructions, she'd better get to her chores. Drat it, her brother Peter had the best of it, going out fishing with their pa while she, because she was a girl, had to stay at home with her mother and tend to the small farm. How she ached to be free of this dull place!

Blossom *was* waiting. She turned her large brown eyes in Adelaide's direction as if to say, "So there you are. 'Tis about time!" She shook her head as Adelaide reached down to wipe off the cow's swollen udder. Adelaide sat down on the small stool, positioned the pail between her knees, and rested her head against the cow's warm flank. It wasn't that she minded milking the cow, feeding the chickens, or working in the family's small vegetable garden. Those were all necessary tasks if they were to survive, and not many families had as much as her family had. Her problem was that doing these jobs gave her time to think—and that was where the danger lay. Adelaide was restless.

Two

Adelaide poured the fresh, steaming milk through a cloth strainer to filter out any loose debris or cow hairs that could have fallen into the pail. Then she poured the strained milk into large, open, flat pans to allow the cream to rise to the top, later to be skimmed off for butter. Blossom's milk had a wonderfully high fat content, and the butter Adelaide churned and sold to the neighbors was her own pin money. Her father often told her, "Every somebody needs his own, and this butter money is yours, Addie."

She covered the pans of milk with clean, soft cloths and went in search of her mother, expecting to find her in the living room, more than likely, sewing. Her mother made all the family's clothing—spent most of her time at it—and left most of the cooking and housework to Adelaide. Adelaide didn't mind too much—better than being sent off to one of the wealthier white families in town to work.

Eager to share her news of the stranger she had seen, she hurried into the front room. Voices stopped her at the door, but not before she had blurted out, "Momma, guess what!"

"Honey, we got company," her mother interrupted.

Adelaide gulped down the flow of words as she saw

the same man she had just seen rise quickly to his feet to greet her with a formal bow.

"Your servant, *Fraulein* . . . er, miss."

His voice was deep and pleasant to hear, Adelaide thought, but the accent was strange to her ears. She'd never heard anything like it before. It was not a Maine accent, to be sure.

"Addie, this here's Alexander Sinclair. You two played together as children. Know you don't remember," her mother said.

"No, I don't, really, but," Adelaide nodded in Alex's direction, "did see him walk up the beach today from the town pier. Came in to tell you."

"Just telling Alexander here 'bout his folks," Mrs. Summers added.

"Can't believe they are dead," Alex murmured. His face mirrored his distress. "I haven't seen them since I was four. Now they're gone. I had not expected such news."

"And I'm truly sorry, son, to be the one givin' it to you," Mrs. Summers said. She noticed how straight and tall Alex stood, as if to absorb the dreadful news more easily.

Alex heard the compassion in the farm woman's voice. She certainly exhibited none of the harsh formality that Frau Erlans and Herr Tiedemann had always shown him. Even his apprentice, master draftsman Herr Steinbach, had treated him formally most of the time. He wasn't accustomed to kindness from a stranger and didn't know quite how to react.

"You want to know what happened, I guess, son. Your ma 'n I was best friends. But after you were taken away, she grieved mightily. Went into decline. Hard, I know, to b'lieve your own folks could send you off."

Adelaide watched Alex's face. She shifted from her position in the doorway and moved to the chair near her father's old desk. She did not take her eyes away from Alex's face. She noticed how he focused his attention on her mother and how he seemed to be almost physically struck by the words as Mrs. Summer spoke them. He moved his head frequently and abruptly, as if trying to deflect the words away from his mind. Adelaide felt sorry for him as her mother continued with the sorrowful litany.

"It was the war, the revolution, fighting them English. Prices was high, taxes on everything, and . . . no work. Even had to fight Indians, sometimes. You know, my own husband, Adelaide's pa, was bound out 'til he was eighteen. Got paid a hundred dollars. That's how he got his fishin' boat 'n this here little farm. Me, myself, only eight when I was sent to live with the Rogers family. Got a cow and a featherbed for my pay. 'Course, we was free . . . my pa even fought in the war . . . but still didn't mean we were better off. No job, no work, even if he did fight 'gainst the English. If it hadn't been for farming 'n fishing, we'd have starved. But to get back to your folks—your pa went off to ship out of Nantucket on a whaler, all colored crew. Came back after a year and a half, almost as empty-handed as when he'd left. Your momma couldn't seem to handle herself. Truly believe her heart was broken, with her baby boy gone."

With an empathetic smile, Mrs. Rachel Summers bobbed her cloth-covered head in Alex's direction. Soft wisps of gray hair showed around the edges. However, it was her plain brown friendly face and her warm smile that intrigued Alex. He'd seen few people of color in Germany, only one or two males, university students from Africa. He recalled their faces were more severe and usually a darker hue than Mrs. Summers'. As he looked from mother to daughter, he wondered what the women of his race were really like.

He addressed Mrs. Summers.

"Thank you, madam, for the information you have given me. I'll be on my way to my parents' home." Hat in hand, he moved to the doorway.

Mrs. Summers raised her hand to stop him.

"No need to hurry there, son. In time you can go . . . in time."

She watched his reaction to her words and saw him nod in agreement.

"You know, I knew exactly who you were when you walked by. Walk just like your pa, but you got your momma's face . . . smooth brown skin, big, round, jet-black eyes that I remember so well. That's why I called to you. Didn't want you to go to an empty house, not alone, anyway."

As Adelaide listened to her mother, she studied their guest. He was quite tall, sturdy, without excess fat. His body was trim, from what she could see by the way his clothes fit. He seemed agile enough, but there was a certain rigidity about his movements, as if he was keeping his body and mind under control.

Her mother's voice interrupted her thoughts.

"Addie," she directed her daughter, "run out to the yard and wring one of the old hens' necks. We'll have fricasseed chicken with dumplings for supper."

She turned to Alex, who had started to protest.

"No, son, you're going to have a meal with us. Least

we can do. My husband and son will be coming in directly, and then we can decide what you should do next. You don't need to see that sorry place until later, when you can catch your breath. Been eighteen years; another day doesn't matter."

While her mother kept the young man entertained in the front room, Adelaide hurriedly prepared the meal. The old hen might have been tough, but Addie had seared the cut pieces in hot fat to keep in the meat juices before she'd placed them in the large iron pot to simmer. When the meat was nearly done, she peeled carrots, potatoes, and onions and put them in the pot, along with two bay leaves. As she worked setting the table in the kitchen, she listened for her father and brother. Should be coming in soon, she thought. Hopefully, they had had a satisfying day and had made a good catch. As usual, they would be starved after a day at sea; she was sure of that. All day out on the ocean gave anyone an appetite, and her brother and father were always famished when they came in from the sea.

Her mind kept wandering back to the stranger in the house. She could hear his odd voice interspersed with her mother's. Evidently her curious mother was encouraging him to talk about himself, because it was his voice Adelaide heard most. She found herself yearning to learn more about Alexander Sinclair. Would his coming to Maine change her life?

She heard footsteps stomping hard outside the kitchen door, and when she turned from the fire where she had been tending to the evening meal, the door burst open and her brother Peter rushed in, bringing a pungent odor of salt air and fish with him.

"Addie! Supper ready? I'm starved!"

"That's nothing new, Pete. You are always starving and . . . dirty. Better wash up. We got company."

"I know. Pa and I brought his suitcases up."

"How come? Whose suitcases?"

"Yep, harbormaster told us somebody named Alexander Sinclair left them, and would Pa bring them to the old Sinclair place. Has he gone over to that old rundown house?" Peter asked.

"Ma wouldn't let him. Told him he'd best eat first, go later. But now," she looked outside the kitchen window, "getting mighty dark outside, don't see how he can. Where's Pa, anyway?"

"He's coming. Giving Samson more feed, I expect."

"Did all right on today's trip?"

"Betcha! Right good haul on cod and pollock. Pa says 'nother good catch like today, he plans on tradin' up to a bigger boat."

Adelaide smiled at that news. Besides being an excellent fisherman, her father was a shrewd trader. That's how he'd gotten the horse and buggy. He'd found a rusty scythe out in the field and had cleaned it up, removed the rust, oiled and sharpened the blade, made a beautiful oak handle with two holders balanced perfectly. The refurbished tool could be swung, and it cut hay with ease. His neighbor, a farmer named Smithson, saw it one day and asked, "What you willin' to take fer that there scythe?"

"What you got to give for it?" her father had replied.

"Brand-new calf," Smithson offered.

"Well, that's fair enough," her father agreed. "Long

as it's healthy." But as the story went, Adelaide remembered her father had traded the calf to a young widow who'd needed a young cow more than she did an old horse and broken-down buggy.

Isaac Summers, wise in his ways, knew he could repair the buggy, and he relished the idea of owning the horse and rig. He figured the horse was a bit long in the tooth, but he'd trade him for a better, healthier, younger one as soon as he had a chance.

"Peter," Adelaide admonished her brother, "you'd better get cleaned up quick. Know how Momma is 'bout having fishy smells in the house."

"Don't know why Ma's so fussy when that's what feeds us," Peter complained.

"You know how Momma is—says we might be poor, but we don't have to be poor and dirty."

"I know if Momma'd had her way, she be anything but a fisherman's wife. Swears *she* was meant to be quality folk."

Adelaide grunted as she fanned her hot face from the fire's heat. "Sometimes I think Momma tries too hard to pattern herself after those white people she used to live with."

"Well, we ain't white, so I don't know why she bothers," her brother said, as he washed his hands and face in the basin of warm water that he had poured. "Pa says be what you are and be proud of that."

"Momma only wants that, too, I believe. It's just that she doesn't want us to be looked down on because of our color."

"Pa says hold your head high and look folks in the eye—then they can't look down on *you*. Ain't that right, Pa?" Peter said to their father, who had arrived carrying two suitcases into the kitchen. He dropped them to the floor and exhaled, relieved of the bags.

"Ain't what right, son? Addie, is there a young man here, come in by boat sometime today?" Isaac Summers' face was flushed from the exertion of carrying the suitcases and the news of his guest.

"In the front room with Momma. Name of Alexander Sinclair."

"God, you mean Molly and Homer's son?"

Adelaide nodded. "I could hardly believe the old harbormaster who said it was Homer Sinclair's son back from Germany. Haven't seen that child since he was four. My God!" He blew out his cheeks.

Adelaide and Peter watched their father. Rarely had they seen him so excited as he rushed into the front room of the house to greet his old friend's son.

Three

Angus Worrell, a Quaker merchant, decided to enter the shipbuilding trade. He recognized that time was extremely important to his business. He was eager to find a faster way to get goods and services from the Old World to the New World.

He told his brother and partner, John, "I want a packet ship that will outdistance the ones the British are using now. Lads up there in Halifax been seeing the wrecks come in—call them 'coffin brigs,' so many of them are foundering at sea. I want a ship that'll stand up to the dastardly winds and rough seas and make headway. You know, John," he told his brother, "there's only one way to make money. That is to be the first with the best."

John Worrell agreed. He had no doubt that his red-haired, self-directed older brother would succeed. He listened intently, aware that whatever Angus put his mind to, he'd never rest until he'd accomplished the goal. As siblings, they had come a long way from Yorkshire, England, selling the cloth manufactured by their father and uncle. Providing woolen cloth in the New World had gained the brothers considerable wealth and acclaim, but Angus saw a promising future in importing and selling the kind of merchandise the colonists needed, and exporting tobacco, cotton, and rum to the Old World. But to do that, he needed his own ship.

"You know, Angus," John offered, "down in Maine, near Portland, I heard there was a black fellow who's rebuilt his folks' house, a draftsman who'd been apprenticed in Germany. You know, the Germans are skilled craftsmen. If this bloke can design a house, he ought to be able to design a ship."

"Aye, could be. And I know what I want."

"First off, I'd say a bigger ship than the packets sailing from England now."

"Right." Angus pulled his pipe from his mouth and leaned forward, elbows on his desk, and using his pipe as a pointer, traced in the air the outline of a ship. "Truly believe more sail, more yardage, and maybe a smoother keel would do the trick."

Back in Stoningham, Alexander Sinclair was thinking much the same thing. His apprenticeship funds were almost depleted, and he was restless. He was a qualified draftsman, but what could he design that would be in demand? He thought about the question that had been put to him by first mate Larkin of the *Emmaline,* the British barque that had returned him to his homeland. Could he really design a clipper ship?

Since his marriage to Adelaide, there was little to keep him busy. He ached to get back to drafting. A fast clipper ship kept crowding into his mind.

"Mr. Summers?" Alex questioned his father-in-law one evening.

"Call me Pa . . . Pa Summers, if you like. Ah, son, you're in the family now."

"Yes, sir . . . Pa Summers . . . I've been thinking. If you could, what would you do to make a boat, or any ship for that matter, move with more speed?"

Isaac Summers heard the serious intent in Alex's voice and he answered thoughtfully. This boy is ambitious, he thought.

"Short and bulky is not going to do it, if you wants speed. Jest look at this here sharpie that I traded up to from my old skiff. Now, I'm not sayin' the skiff was no good, but that old flat-bottomed boat wasn't built fer speed. But now, this sharpie here, *Mary Anne,* she's still flat-bottomed, same's the skiff, but she's long and narrow, 'n' the centerboard steadies her, 'specially when I get the sails up 'n she takes in the wind."

"Think I see. It's shape and sails."

"Yep, you got to remember what moves a ship is the wind, 'n fer that you need cloth, many sails, to catch the wind."

"The shape should be . . ."

Isaac pointed, "Son, look at that there fish in the bottom of the pail. Look at that shape . . . built for speed, he is. Can cut through the water. Look at a turtle. His shape ain't exactly built fer speed."

"Agreed!" Alex's face lit up with excitement at the new knowledge.

"Pa Summers, with your help, I think I can design such a craft. Sleek enough to cut through the waters and skip over the waves rather than plow through them, with enough sail to catch even the slightest breeze."

" 'Twould need a tall mast, perhaps two or three, with special riggin' to handle the lines. Can you do that?"

Alex nodded thoughtfully. Isaac Summers saw determination in his son-in-law's serious face.

The sun was drifting toward the horizon, and the fishermen edged their boat toward the shoreline and home. Alex's eyes burned from the radiance of sea and sun. He shaded them with his hands.

"My apprentice master," he told Isaac, "said if you can see in your mind what you want, you can have it. I can see such a ship. She would be fleet, slender, designed to fly over the ocean waves, gather the winds close to her bosom, and yield to no one."

Noting the serious, thoughtful tone in Alex's voice, Isaac responded admiringly, "Son, you sound like a poet or a dreamer . . . don't know which."

"Perhaps, but I aim to be a ship designer. From what that first mate told me, the time for faster ships is now. You will help me?"

"Said I would. Winter's comin' on, give us something to do, pass the time away."

And Alex thought, the Sinclair name will mean something at last.

Four

As Alex explained to Angus Worrell, "You need a ship that will 'clip over' the waves, not plow through them." And he added, "The weight and center of gravity must be considered."

Angus Worrell was delighted when he viewed Alex's ship designs, but his eyes nearly left his head when he saw the complete model of the ship that Alex had placed on his desk.

Her hull was jet-black, and a white stripe bordered her sides. Inside the hull, gleaming panels of oak and pine created a handsome interior. The cotton sails made by Rachel Summers could be manipulated by ropes and riggings—even a replica of an anchor hung from its locker under the fo'c'sle.

"I call her *Belle Adele,* sir, for my beautiful wife, Adelaide."

"I'd agree that was appropriate," the merchant concurred.

Alex, warmed to his subject, went on, "I propose, sir, that the flaring bow you see here," he pointed to the front end of the model, "the longer bowsprit and finer end, will allow more sail. It's the vast amount of sail that will be needed to haul more wind. Of course, that means taller masts, especially the mainmast."

"How tall a mast?"

"Oh, I'd say at least one hundred thirty feet, which means more men to work the sails, so the ship will have to accommodate not only crew, but any passengers you wish to carry."

"So you think . . ." Mr. Worrell persisted.

"A ship over two hundred feet on the keel, and about two hundred fifty feet on deck."

"Copper-bottomed."

"Oh, yes, copper-bottomed, must do everything possible to protect the keel from the ship worm."

"About how many decks?"

"I'd say three as I've shown here in the model, with a quarterdeck abaft and a forecastle, a higher deck forward, with a poop deck, higher deck aft."

"What excites me, young man," Angus said, his face flushed with excitement, "is the yardage you've shown for the sails."

"It's what you'll need for speed, sir. A full-rigged ship, three masts, fore and aft sails, with a flying jib connected to the longer bowsprit."

"Beautiful, beautiful." Angus Worrell rubbed his hands. "I believe you've done it! Can you, will you, sell me your design and your model? I must have this ship built."

Going right to the point, he asked, "What do I owe you?" His eyes never left Alex's face.

Alex had already looked around the merchant's plain but prosperous-looking office. The walls were of heavy oak, and the wide-planked floor was smooth pine. A silver tea set graced a console against the far wall. Apparently, the Worrell brothers continued their English custom of afternoon tea. Alex had observed the man's expensive woolen suit and realized that he was dealing with a wealthy as well as astute businessman. All he had was his skill as a draftsman. He had thought long about his ability and was determined to do his best.

"Mr. Worrell," Alex answered slowly, as he engaged the merchant with steady eye contact, "as you have heard, I was apprenticed to a German master craftsman until I was eighteen. But I am a free man of color."

"I know, I know. As a Quaker, I have no problem."

"Please allow me to continue, sir. I intend to make my living as a draftsman. So . . . I will sell you my design and model for a fixed sum, two hundred dollars . . ."

"Fine, fine," Angus Worrell agreed.

"But hear me out, sir, please. The design and model will be yours, but in addition, I must have a five-percent interest in any ships built from my designs. I will also offer you the first opportunity to bid on my future designs. I have a wife to support, and we are expecting our first child."

The merchant moved from behind his desk to shake Alex's hand.

"I see you have confidence in your ship's design. I like that, and I like a man who comes right to the point. My lawyer will have the contract ready tomorrow. The war has been difficult for all of us, but now it is time to move ahead."

The mail arrived a few days later with a contract and extra bonus check for Mr. Alexander Sinclair, Master Draftsman.

Part Two

Five

Alexander Sinclair smiled at his young daughter as he pulled her into his lap. She settled in comfortably, secure in her father's arms as he sat in the great chair in front of the blazing fireplace.

"Liebchen," he said, "now that you are six, you must start school. Tomorrow will be your first day . . ."

"But Papa," Zevia interrupted, a firm pout on her lips, "do I have to? I want to be here, at home, with you. I *never* want to leave you."

Her father held his daughter close for a moment, then he pulled playfully at her thick braids.

"Little one, I know you don't *want* to leave me, but you must learn."

"But," she insisted, "I only want to draw ships, like you do . . ."

Alexander nodded over the child's head, his heart pained with thoughts of the future of his motherless child. His poor wife Adelaide had survived only a few moments after their daughter's birth.

"You must learn more than how to draw ships," he told her. "Someday you will have to stand on your own two feet. We have to prepare you for that day."

"You mean, I won't be with you . . . and Oma and Opa?"

"The day will come, *Liebchen*," he spoke firmly, "when your grandparents and I won't be around. We want to be sure that you can make your way in the world."

"Yes, Papa," Zevia sighed. She knew the matter was settled.

"Come," her father stood, "let us clean and polish your shoes. You must be neat and tidy, like a proper school-girl."

"Every night we polish shoes, Papa. Must we tonight?" Zevia complained.

"Indeed, yes! Every night we clean away the dirt from the day's work, and we start fresh each morning with clean, polished shoes to step out into the world and face whatever it brings."

That first week at school had brought taunts and jeers. Zevia walked slowly down the dirt road. She kicked at the dust and stones along the way. She had just had another fight with some of her classmates after school. Perhaps after today, they'd leave her alone.

Every day that first week, her schoolmates continued to call her names. The only colored girl in the school, she knew she was singled out, and as her grandmother had warned her, "They goin' to make fun of you 'cause of your color, but remember, God made you—hold your head high." Her grandmother didn't know they were going to call Zevia "dirty Heinie."

She picked up a stone, heaved it at a tree, and was pleased with the loud *thunk* the stone made as it hit the trunk. She wished it could have been the head of Molly

Menlo, the ringleader, who had started the teasing name-calling.

Zevia reflected as she made her way up the knoll along the oceanside toward home that perhaps the whole thing had been her fault. She should never have let on that she could speak German. What had possessed her to do it, anyway, that first day of school? She couldn't explain, even now, a week later, why she had responded to the teacher the way she had. Somehow, the need to be special had overwhelmed her and she couldn't stop herself. She would never forget the amazed look on the stern, unfriendly face of Miss MacAllston when Zevia had answered roll call that first school morning.

"And what is your name?" the teacher had asked as she'd come to stand at Zevia's desk, her chart and pen ready to inscribe the student's name on the seating plan.

Zevia looked up at the woman, and without a moment's hesitation, responded, *"Ich heibe Zevia. Zevia Sinclair. Wie heiben sie?"*

In the silence that followed, the whole class seemed to draw in a collective breath. The hiss could be heard all over the room. Miss MacAllston's face had flushed an explosive red when she'd realized that this little colored girl had shown the audacity to ask for *her* name—in German!

A nervous giggle rippled through the room from some of the students, but Zevia didn't care. She didn't blink an eye, but merely waited for the teacher's reaction. What if she *was* the only Negro child in the elementary school in Stoningham, Maine? She had something none of the others had, a father who spoke German . . . and had insisted that she learn to speak it as well.

"You never know, *Liebchen,* when the knowledge will

come in handy. Never can tell when you may have to use it," he had said to her. Her father had taught her to read the language as well.

"Don't you think you're makin' this child study too much?" her grandmother Rachel had protested to her son-in-law.

"No, Oma. As colored people, we need to know all we can to make it," her father had said.

So the lessons had continued.

Zevia could see that the teacher was made momentarily speechless by her student's revelation.

"How come you can speak German?"

"My papa taught me," Zevia said.

"Your father is German? You don't look German."

"Nein . . . I mean, no, my papa grew up in Germany."

"I see. And your mother?"

"My momma is dead," Zevia answered quietly.

"Oh, well," the teacher poised her pen over her chart, "you say your name is Zevia Sinclair?"

"Papa said my momma named me before she died," Zevia had announced. There was pride in her voice. She knew, *somehow,* that her name was unusual, and she reveled that it helped make her special. Maybe that's why her mother had given her the name—so she'd be special. Zevia knew she wanted that feeling now more than ever.

Now her dress was torn, the waistline almost completely ripped. She had to hold the skirt bunched in her left hand. Her hair was mussed up from the blows of Molly Menlo, a dark-haired Italian fisherman's daughter who had grabbed her and led the taunting jeers of the other students.

"Dirty Heinie, you're a dirty Heinie," the scoffing ridicule continued until Zevia, angered beyond control, fought back valiantly. She hit out blindly with her only weapon, her book bag. She struck Molly Menlo on the head. She heard her dress rip as she struggled out of the grasp of the bigger girl. Molly Menlo, still holding onto Zevia's skirt, fell to the ground, momentarily stunned. The other children ran from the scene.

From the ground where she lay, Molly Menlo glared at Zevia disbelieving, amazed she had been hit, that the little colored girl would dare strike her.

"Now," Zevia pronounced in a firm voice, "now maybe you'll leave me alone!" She turned on her heel and marched home without a backward glance.

She hoped she'd be able to slip into the house without being seen. Her grandmother would be angry about the torn dress. Could she hide it until she could mend it herself? Usually Oma was in the front room sewing, working on another quilt, no doubt, and her father was in his study at the back of the house, working on his newest ship designs. Opa, her beloved grandfather, would be coming in from his fishing trip later that day. Just as well, she thought, in her present fix there would be no one to welcome her home. But, somehow, it seemed to her on days like this one she longed for the comforting circle of a mother's arms.

Zevia knew she was loved by her family. Her grandparents had come to live with them after she was born. Her father had enlarged the house with bedrooms upstairs. Her uncle Peter was married and on his own, but there was still this large hole in her heart caused by her motherless state. Each of her classmates had a mother. How was it she could miss what she had never had? She wondered, was she destined always to live with that vacuum in her life?

She quietly let herself into the kitchen, careful not to let the screen door slam, and she crept past the living room door, where she saw her grandmother bent over her sewing. Silently, she went to her room and changed her dress. She stuffed the torn garment in the corner of her closet.

She told no one about the fight.

"Had a good day at school?" her grandmother asked her, when Zevia helped with the supper meal.

"Yes, Oma, a good day," was her answer.

Later, after the dishes had been washed, the kitchen tidied up, she went to her father's study, where she knew he'd be working. It was his evening habit; he said there were not enough hours in the day to do all he wanted to do. Zevia admired his ambition.

"Papa?"

"Yes, *Liebling,* what is it?" Her father took his pipe from his mouth and smiled at her. Encouraged, Zevia plunged into her question.

"Papa, why did my mother die? Did I make her die . . . by being born?"

She heard her father sigh, saw him place his drawing pencil on top of his drafting table. He bent down to hug her. His face was on a level with hers, and Zevia saw the pain in his dark eyes. His voice was soft and quiet as he tried to answer his child's question.

"Zevia, *Liebling.*" Zevia could sense the stress her father felt, and she felt badly about that, but she had to have an answer to her question.

"Liebling, I loved your momma with all my heart, and I know she loved me, too. Of course you did not make

her die! Never think such a thing! She wanted you, I wanted you . . . we both wanted you. She even named you. But we will never know why she died. The doctor did not know. We miss her, Oma, Opa, and I, and we always will, but we do have you, *Liebchen*. Just be the best little girl in the world, that's all we ask."

"But Papa, suppose I can't be the best little girl in the whole world?" Zevia asked, mindful of her school escapade.

"Ach! But you can be, Zevia, if you put your mind to it. You can be, I've no doubt of that. You're my independent, fearless *Fraulein*. I know you will be able to do whatever you wish."

Her father hugged her briefly, stood up, and turned to his work. Not satisfied with her father's response, Zevia had wanted to remain in his embrace longer, exult in the strength of his arms, breathe in not only the aroma of his tobacco smell, but reinforce her own value by somehow capturing the aura of her father's self-esteem. But as quickly as her father immersed himself in his work at the drafting table, Zevia felt she was forgotten, not secure, even with her father's pronouncement of her innocence in her mother's death. The only thing she was really sure of was that the void in her heart seemed larger.

Later that evening, after Zevia had gone to bed, Alex Sinclair joined his in-laws in the living room. Mrs. Summers was still sewing. Her husband worked on a ship model beside the kerosene lamp on the other side of the table.

Alex took a large chair and pulled it up to face the

fireplace where the burning wood crackled and flamed, sending warmth into the room.

"Zevia asked me tonight why her mother died," Alex announced.

"Oh, no, she did?" Rachel Summers responded quickly. "What did you tell her?"

"That she was not to blame . . . it wasn't her fault . . ."

"I'll never forget the day that child was born," Rachel reflected with a sigh. "Started out to be such a lovely summer day. Bright, sunny, beautiful, with the bluest sky I've ever seen in my life. Such promise. And it ended . . ."

"With our hearts broken," Alex said.

"You two ought not to talk like that. Think about Zevia, what she needs," Mr. Summers interjected.

"But why did Adelaide have to die? Why didn't she, couldn't she, fight to keep on living? Why?" Alex's voice cracked momentarily as he sought answers.

"I wonder many times, whatever did I do to make her like that?" Rachel Summers said. "Often, as a child, she would go off by herself to sit on the rocks and gaze at the ocean. I never knew what she was looking for."

Rachel's eyes misted as she talked, and she turned to look at Alex. Now, close to forty, he was still a strikingly good-looking man. Tall, straight, his body as wiry and lean as ever, his black hair now tinged with gray at the temples. He bore the tragedies of his life with stoic patience. However, his eyes flicked with happiness whenever he looked at his daughter.

"I do know one thing, Mother S. I will always have this raging, howling storm deep inside my heart," he said. "Because I truly loved. your daughter. Perhaps I didn't show her, let her know, but . . ." he sighed.

"I know, son, know you tried. My child was a person with her own private demons deep in her soul, I guess. Nothing we could do to help her."

Alex shook his head sadly, his eyes clouded by the memory of the day his daughter was born.

The Sinclair family fortunes had risen with Alexander Sinclair becoming a much-sought-after ship designer. He had designed not only packet ships for the Worrell Brothers, but had designed a clipper ship, the *Eastern Queen,* that had even more speed than the small packet ships. The War of 1812 had enriched the woolen fortunes of the Worrells, and Alex's five-percent interest had yielded substantial dividends for him. He had added a large room, complete with skylights, to the rear of the house, an office of his own, plus room for several apprentice-students to whom he was teaching the crafts of drafting and designing. He was working there that beautiful morning when Adelaide went into labor.

Now, at last, his dreams of a family of his own would come true. The Sinclair name would be carried on, nobly, by the son about to be born.

The doctor and the midwife had been summoned. Alex could afford both, wanted his wife to have the best, and it was planned that the midwife would remain for the first week or so of Adelaide's confinement.

The wait proved not to be very long, Dr. Baldwin explained later.

"Your wife was unusually quiet, I noticed, for someone about to deliver. That concerned me. But finally she had a strong urge to push. I encouraged her to do so, and within a few seconds your baby was born. When I showed the baby to your wife, she said, very quietly, 'What is it?' 'A lovely little girl, Mrs. Sinclair,' I said.

'Good,' she said. 'Her name is Zevia.' Then she turned her face to the wall, took a deep breath, and there was nothing, *nothing,* I, any of us, could do. She was gone. And . . . she never looked at the baby, never held her. I'm so sorry."

Alex would never forget the distress and sadness he saw that day on Dr. Baldwin's face. For years afterward the doctor remarked that losing a young mother, especially in childbirth, was the most devastating, horrifying experience in a doctor's life.

Six

Zevia paced her bedroom floor. As she walked back and forth across the room, her mind worried and troubled, she did not see the colorful bed quilt her grandmother had sewn for her, did not see her doll collection, nor the stuffed animals that her father had lavished on her during her childhood. She was oblivious to the bookcase lined with her favorite books, the crisp white curtains at the windows, or the soft wool carpet, with its muted colors, under her feet.

She felt only the thumping, wild beat of her heart as it echoed the thundering waves that crashed on the shoreline below the knoll. She stopped in front of the window that faced the ocean and looked out at the angry waves that raged against the beach. All morning her thoughts had returned to the previous year, the year her innocence was stolen.

Her father said, "Now that you've finished elementary school, I want you to go to school in Boston, *Liebchen*. Your education needs to be finished, rounded out, so to speak."

He showed her a pamphlet that he'd retrieved from the pile of papers on his desk. "See, here it is, the Boston Academy, run by the African Free Female Society."

"You're sending me away, Papa?" Zevia's eyes widened at the news.

"I must, *Liebchen*. You are coming into young womanhood. You are nearly fourteen." His face broke into a grin. *"Ach,* see," he pulled her to stand beside him, "you are almost as tall as your poor old papa here. It will be only for a few years that you will be away, then I suspect the young lads will come calling on my Miffy." He kissed her cheek.

"Papa, I'm *not* interested in boys."

"We shall see, Miffy," her father said. "We shall see."

As she moved restlessly around her bedroom, her mind returned to the days of self-discovery in Boston. She had not planned to fall in love with Walton Springer, but she had. So she knew she must leave home again, this time perhaps for the final time. Tears welled in her eyes as she looked out at the ocean. She could almost hear the waves accuse her of her dreadful mistaken judgment. She did not know how she could survive, but survive she must. She could not bring disgrace to the Sinclair name.

Boston's city streets, especially around the college campuses, were active that spring. The students had been cloistered all winter long and were delighted with their new freedom from winter snows, the blustery northeast winds that it seemed had buffeted them almost daily that winter. Students swarmed the sidewalks after their classes, sought some springtime diversion. The school year was almost over.

Zevia and her roommate, Victoria Freeman, a student from New York City, were like all the others. Zevia felt the excitement and lightheartedness that the balmy, soft weather brought to Boston.

The two girls often walked in the evening from their school in the South End, down Massachusetts Avenue, across Memorial Bridge, over the Charles River into Cambridge. That was when Victoria spied the sign outside Saint Andrew's Episcopal Church.

"Look, Zev!" Victoria pointed to the church bulletin board, "They're having a church supper tomorrow night. Says, 'Public Invited.' Let's go! Might meet somebody. God knows it's been a dull winter. I'm ready for some excitement. There's been little or none of it at school. What do you say?"

"Well, all right, I guess," Zevia answered. "Be going home soon, anyway. May as well . . . might be interesting."

The next night, Victoria went off at once with a young man who'd invited her to sit with him at supper.

Zevia found herself being approached by a tall, light-skinned man with slicked-back hair. He wore a clerical collar that to Zevia's unsophisticated eye seemed to enhance his good looks with a beautific sanctity. He introduced himself as Walton Springer, an assistant to the rector, studying at the divinity school.

"Zevia Sinclair," Zevia said, as she accepted his handshake.

"Welcome to Saint Andrew's, Miss Sinclair," he responded.

Zevia found her hand enclosed by soft fingers. She was drawn like a moth to a flame, almost without a will of her own, encompassed totally by the magnetism of the man.

That spring, before she knew what had happened, she

fell hopelessly in love with Walton Springer. Walton pursued her diligently. Zevia had never known such happiness. She told him so one night as he walked her to the roominghouse where she and Victoria lived with other students.

"I never knew, Walton, that I could feel this way. I am so happy!" Her eyes sparkled with joy, and Walton drew her closer to him, his arm around her shoulder as they walked.

"You know, Zevia, you are the love of my life. I want to marry you—be with you forever."

Zevia stopped walking and turned to face him.

"You really mean that, Walton?"

"I do, my dear, with all my heart."

"Then you'll have to come to Maine and meet my family."

"Your family?"

"Yes, my papa, my Oma and Opa . . ."

"Oma, Opa?" Walton questioned. "Oh, you mean your grandparents. I shall be delighted to meet your family," Walton said smoothly.

"I speak German, too," Zevia announced proudly. "Do you speak German?"

"Oh, my God, no! I don't speak any language 'cept English." He looked down on her, a broad smile on his handsome face. "Think your father will approve of me?"

Impulsively, Zevia hugged him.

"My father will love you because we love each other, Walton. Have no fear."

"Then it's settled. We'll go to Maine to meet your family as soon as school closes."

"Oh, Walton, you make me so happy! I can hardly

wait! The next few months will just drag by, I know it."

Fleetingly, she wondered if Walton could sense her naked desire for him. Did that make her a bad woman? She didn't care. Her fierce longing, the void in her heart, would be filled.

Zevia could not explain her happiness. She was loved by a real man who wanted her. She stored the secret in her heart. Oh, Victoria knew the couple were together a lot, but she was busy with her own relationship. And Zevia could not explain to anyone why she did not talk about her serious affair with Walton. Somehow, she felt if she talked about it, it would disappear. So she kept her counsel, lived for the moments when they could be together.

She would walk to the church, attend the activities Walton had charge of—the young people's groups, choir rehearsals, the women's guild, the deacon and trustee meetings, and then Walton would walk her home at night. She treasured these moments.

One evening he suggested she should see where he lived. Naive and trusting, Zevia allowed him to take her to his apartment on a small street in the South End.

"You should know where I live, my love, because you never know . . . I'd want to be able to help you if ever, God forbid, you were in need. You need to know how to reach me. Always try the church offices first. If I'm not there, I'll be here," he lied smoothly. He did not tell her he had borrowed the apartment for the night.

Zevia accepted his reasoning, and as hard as she tried to push her doubts aside, somehow, she couldn't stop herself from placing her hand trustingly in his and allowing him to lead her up the stairs of the brownstone.

He loves me, she kept telling herself. He's a religious man, he won't do anything to hurt me . . . he loves me. He said so. I do believe him.

He walked her home later that evening. He was as loving, sweet, and caring as he had always been, but Zevia wondered, how was it she felt so bruised and used? No one had told her she would feel this way. Suddenly, she felt a hole open in her heart. She wasn't loved at all. The emptiness was still there.

Walton insisted that their plans to go to Maine were still in the offing. He had purchased the train tickets.

"We'll leave right after Sunday services are over, Zevia. And we'll be in Stoningham later that evening."

Zevia said she would be packed and ready when he came to pick her up to go to the train station.

That night, when one of the girls in the roominghouse told her she had a visitor, Zevia couldn't imagine who it was. It happened on Saturday night, the day before she was to return home. She never saw Walton on Saturday or Sunday because, as he said, "There's too much church business I must be involved with."

"For me?" she asked.

"Said Zevia Sinclair—seemed to know you live here," the student said.

"A man or a woman?" Zevia questioned.

"Oh, it's a woman."

Zevia hurried downstairs to the living room. That's when she saw her visitor.

Zevia gasped, clasped her hand to her mouth. She noticed at once the young woman's ponderous belly, the dark, misshapen coat that barely closed over the pregnancy. Dark eyes stared out at Zevia from a small, pinched brown face. Zevia could see that if not pregnant, the girl would be rail thin. Intuitively, Zevia knew that her own immediate future was about to change.

"Are you Zevia Sinclair? Must be, because you fit the description given to me. My name is Maybelle Springer. Walton Springer is my husband, and our first child is expected next month." She glared at Zevia. "That's all I got to say."

The room spun wildly and Zevia stood transfixed, her hands to her mouth to keep her screams of disbelief from hurtling out. She did not wait to see the woman leave, but ran rapidly up the stairs to her room.

Early the next day she took the Sunday excursion boat from Boston to Portland, Maine.

Zevia's thoughts returned to the present. She never wanted anyone to know how vulnerable she'd been, and she promised herself she'd never be so weak again. Not for any man!

The Portland *Daily Examiner* listed the advertisement on its front page. The notice appeared in italic print in the lower right hand corner of the first page of the paper, close by the column of ships' arrivals and departures.

Wanted: Experienced teacher for young female to travel to China.
Expected length of voyage six to ten months. $50 a month.

Ref. req. Respond to Capt. Webster Loring,
　Wright's Pier, Portland, Maine.

Alex Sinclair raged, uncharacteristically, at his daughter when she told him of her plans to answer the advertisement.

"Damn it, Zevia, if I thought I could do it, I'd lash you to a post in the cellar, by God, to keep you from doing such a foolish thing! You're out of your head!"

Zevia saw the cords of anger that stood out from her father's forehead. His dark eyes bulged from their sockets in disbelief that his only child would dare defy him.

"You're my only child and now you want to do *what?* Go off to *China?*"

Zevia knew that her father, who had always given her anything she wanted, this time was almost provoked to strike her. She stood her ground and challenged him with an unflinching stare.

"Papa, I've made up my mind to answer this notice. I must! I just can't sit here in Stoningham and wait for life to find me! I just can't!"

Only Zevia knew how sordid, how impure she felt after her Boston experience. She felt Walton was the love of her life. He was so handsome. He had lightly tanned skin and dark, smooth hair, and his gentle touch had melted any reservations she'd felt about becoming involved with him.

She had trusted Walton, had believed he loved her and that she loved him when she'd allowed him to make love to her. It was so exciting, such a thrilling experience for the small-town girl. Why had it all gone wrong?

Now her only redemption lay in not bringing shame on her father and grandparents.

Her father stared at her, not believing her words.

"Zevia, your wish for independence will be the death of me! How can you think of leaving home? I thought when your grandmother and I let you go to Boston to the Academy run by the African Free Female Society . . ."

"But, Papa . . ."

"What is it?" Alex's voice rose even higher in anger. "What is it? You have Oma, your grandmother, who loves you, and me . . . you have Opa, your grandfather. I'd give my life for you. What do you want?"

Feeling that her chance for freedom might be slipping away, Zevia burst out angrily, "My life, Papa, that's what I want! My life!"

Zevia wished she could have bitten her tongue before she'd let the words out. Her father's face blanched visibly under his brown skin. She swallowed nervously when she saw the quickening tears in his eyes.

"Oh, Papa." She moved closer to him. "I don't mean to hurt you. Please, please, I have to do this . . . find my own life."

She pushed herself into his arms and lay her head on his chest. The tears fell onto her hair as silently her father looked over her head, through the long windows of the living room, to the wide ocean beyond the knoll. He knew he could not keep his strong-willed daughter from facing her own future. But why did she have to go so far from him?

Zevia listened to the strong beat of her father's heart as she pressed her face into his woolen vest. It was warm and reassuring, but all the same, she was determined her father would never know the truth. She would never damage the proud Sinclair name.

Zevia's answer to the captain's query was brief and to the point.

Captain Webster Loring
Wright's Pier
Portland, Maine

Dear Captain Loring:
In response to your advertisement, I offer my services to you. I am twenty years old, a free Negro woman with the following qualifications. I graduated from public school and received further education at the Academy for African Free Females in Boston. I was judged to be proficient in all my studies, as well as at the pianoforte. I have read the classics and have studied French and Latin. I also speak German.
For references, I refer you to the Baldwin and Swasey families of Boston and Portland.
My father is a draftsman, and I know the difference between a jib and a topsail.
I await your reply.
(Miss) Zevia Sinclair, Stoningham, Maine.

Captain Loring read the last two sentences of Zevia's letter with a wry smile on his face. Miss Zevia Sinclair seemed like a feisty one, he'd give her that. Besides, he'd had only one other response, from a widow in her forties. He rather doubted she could withstand the rigors of a trip to China. It didn't matter to him that the young woman was a Negro. So were his first mate, the cook-steward, and the cook's wife. The three had been on previous trips with him. He'd had no quarrel with either their work or their loyalty. Since his wife Mary's death six months before, Captain Loring had had to have his seven-year-old daughter, Jane, with him. He could not leave her home with only servants to look after her.

He told his first mate, Sam Cross, about his decision. A dark scowl crossed the young man's face.

"Are you sure, Captain, that such a thing is wise?"

"Sam, my daughter is the most important person left in my life. I have to have her with me, at least, while I can. And it may interest you to know that I've engaged a young Negress." The captain cast a sidelong glance at his first mate, whose reaction was instantaneous. "You might find she's wife material, Sam."

Sam shook his head vehemently.

"Oh, no. Don't try setting me up with a schoolteacher! A wife is the last thing I want—a nagging, screeching she-witch. Oh, no, Captain! You keep your daughter's schoolteacher below decks and out o' my bailiwick, and things'll be just fine!"

"Ah, Sam," Captain Loring said with a chuckle, "you don't know what a real woman's love is like. When it hits you, you'll fall flat on your face—like everyone else."

"Don't want to know," Sam insisted. "My life is just fine, happy, long's I can sail the seven seas with you and the crew. A good ship, the seas, the stars, the adventure are all I'm asking."

Captain Loring's written reply to Zevia Sinclair informed her of a sailing date:

Plan to leave from South Street in New York in two weeks. Bring clothing suitable for warm as well as cold climates.

Alex grunted when Zevia showed him the letter.

"Ah, you will not go to New York alone. Just as the good captain has concern for his daughter, he must know that I have concern for you, my Miffy," he told her.

She had tearful goodbyes for her grandparents. "Know I'll never see you again, child," her grandmother told her, before Zevia and Alex boarded the stage for Boston, where they would pick up another for New York.

Zevia's feelings during the long, uncomfortable ride ranged from fear and apprehension to anger at herself for yielding to the philandering Walton Springer.

Zevia wondered, was her submission to Walton a real weakness on her part? Was she too easily led by Walton's seductive appearance, his quiet thoughtfulness, his involvement in the ministry, the clerical collar he wore? But he had kept the truth from her. Would she ever trust another man? She was glad she was going to China. The next few months might be difficult, but she would meet whatever challenges life sent her way. She would never submit to another man again, she vowed—*never.*

The last night before reaching New York, her father took her hands in his as they sat at dinner in the Flagstaff Inn on the Connecticut Turnpike. Her father fixed his gaze on her face as if he needed to etch it in his brain.

"Liebchen, you do not have to do this. Say the word and we will go back home to Maine. Eh? Say it and we go!"

"Papa, you know I must find my own life, of my own choosing . . ."

"Even if again your papa's heart is breaking at losing his child . . ."

"Please, Papa, you know I love you with all my heart. If you love me, you'll let me go."

"If I love you? If I love you and it kills me to let you go? *Ach, Liebling,* you don't know how much you mean to me, my only child."

Zevia had to call upon all her reserves of strength to keep from weakening, but she knew she loved her father too much to bring shame to him, a man of color, steeled by his need for perfection. She could not, would not, hurt this honorable man. He had suffered enough, and his pride would be shattered, she knew, if he ever found out about her "mistake." "Never forget who you are," he used to say. "Be proud of your name." Did she have any pride left? she wondered. She had never known her mother. Would her life have been much more different if her mother had lived?

Seven

China

When Alex Sinclair took a good look at the *Eastern Queen,* his heart quickened with a deep thrill: he realized it was a ship built from his own design. He gripped his daughter's hand in his and she responded with a firm grasp of her own.

"Ach, Miffy," he said, reverting to her childhood name as he looked at the tall clipper ship that would carry his daughter to the Far East. "It's a Worrell-built vessel of my design!"

He smiled at her, drew her closer. "My poor heart is eased a bit now, seeing you'll be traveling on this vessel that I, your papa, had a hand in creating."

"See, Papa, 'tis a good omen. It will be like being with you, don't you see?" she said hopefully.

"I'd really rather have you home, but alas, I am saddled with a stubborn, hardheaded child." He shook his head.

The ship looked every inch a queen, with a gleaming yellow wooden hull, a dark blue keel, and blue trim around her gunports. Her very long bowsprit pushed proudly toward the heavens as she swung easily, anchored at the wharf.

The excitement of the quay was palpable, and Zevia

had all she could do to keep up with her father as he was swept up in the drama of the crowded, active dock. There were warships, merchant vessels, packets, smaller yawls, several brigs, schooners, and barkentines. There were hordes of men. Sailors from many nations, dock-hands, military men, busy merchants, and businessmen all moved about and jostled one another good-naturedly as they went about their many and varied affairs. The harbor was alive with flags of different countries, spar-kling in the breeze as the ships, like racehorses at the starting gate, restlessly rode the tides, eager to be on their way to some promising destination. They would not be stilled until they had reached their goal of a foreign port and returned home, richer and wiser for the venture.

Zevia looked at her father and realized that the excite-ment was beginning to affect him. He was certainly a prosperous man, with his tall, dark hat, woolen suit, spar-kling white shirt, and his best pearl cufflinks.

"Wouldn't do for Captain Loring to think you're some poor down-easter from the Maine woods," he had told her, when he'd insisted on meeting her employer. "Not *my* daughter."

Now he looked about, his eyes searching. "Got to find a 'jack-tar' to get your trunk aboard."

The smell of the salt air pricked at Zevia's nose as she maneuvered her cautious way around coils of ropes, boxes, and barrels of cargo that waited dockside to be placed on board.

With one hand she held her long skirts free from the dusty wharf and tucked her other hand safely under her father's strong arm as he steered her to the *Eastern Queen*'s gangplank.

They were halted by a young sailor who saluted smartly as they approached.

"This is Miss Zevia Sinclair, the governess-teacher Captain Loring is expecting," Alex told him. "Will you please inform your captain that she has arrived?"

The young man said he would do so at once and bounded up the gangplank to deliver the message.

That was when first mate Sam Cross saw Zevia. He had been standing on the main deck when he'd observed the couple approach the young sailor. He took special note of the pair. Not many people of color who appeared on the dock were well-dressed or looked so prosperous as the pair who caught his attention. The man was distinctive in his appearance: alert, aware of the stares he and the attractive young woman were receiving; but he seemed not in the least disconcerted by the curious glances. It was as if he was accustomed to being singled out.

Next, Sam Cross focused his attention on the young woman. She wore a large framed bonnet that shielded most of her face. She wore a black grosgrain cloak with gray satin lapels and cuffs. Black lace gloves covered her hands, and she carried a black leather purse. A thick roll of long black curls peeked out from the back of her bonnet, and Sam could not help but notice her trim figure, all the way down to her feet, encased in high-buttoned shoes.

So this was the teacher for the captain's daughter, he realized, when the sailor gave him the message. He walked down the gangplank. He was eager to see her face.

"First mate Samuel E. Cross at your service, sir." He saluted Alex, who responded with his customary heel click and bow. He introduced Zevia after a firm hand-shake had been exchanged.

"I am Alexander Sinclair, and this is my daughter, Miss Zevia Sinclair. Captain Loring is not available?"

Sam heard in Alex's voice a certain tone that indicated Mr. Sinclair was accustomed to dealing with preeminent persons, but the first mate took no umbrage. He was second-in-command, for now, but he knew that someday he would have a ship under his own command.

He answered Alex, showing the proper amount of deference and respect. He nodded at Zevia.

"How do you do, Miss Sinclair? To answer your question, sir, the captain is attending to final business, arrangements at the shipping office, but he's expecting Miss Sinclair."

"*Ja,* well, it is important that I meet with him before leaving my daughter."

"He will be here before long. We plan to sail on the evening tide. Our cargo had been loaded, passengers will begin arriving with the hour, and at the very last, fresh provisions will be brought on board," Sam said.

"I will wait," Alex nodded. "Meanwhile, my daughter's trunk must be brought aboard."

Sam heard the distinctive German accent in Alex's voice and noted as well the protective air he exhibited around his daughter. He answered quickly.

"Aye, sir, that will be done at once."

He gestured to a passing sailor who sprang to attention. Eager to please the first mate, the young tar followed Alex to the spot on the quay where the horse-drawn cab driver stood guard over Zevia's possessions.

Left alone with the first mate, Zevia turned her attentions to him.

His skin was a deep copper brown, probably, she thought, from long exposure to the elements. He wore a snowdrift-white shirt with gold shoulderboards indicating his rank. His white trousers outlined the trim, lithe musculature of his legs. Under his cap, dark hair curled around his ears, and the eyes that met hers were dark and introspective. Zevia was acutely aware that the first mate was giving her close scrutiny as well. He doesn't like me, she thought.

She turned her back to him to watch the progress of her trunk being hauled aboard. The excitement and bustling activity of the busy seaport fascinated her. She knew, she hoped, that at last, a new world had opened its arms to her. She would hope for the best. The sounds of unfurled sails snapping against their riggings, yearning to be free; the shouts of the men and the noises of laboring horses as they bent to move cargo filled the air around her. The sight of men climbing up and down thick ropes, seemingly without the slightest fear, fascinated her. For her, every quivering nerve, every responsive cell in her body, seemed more acute, more aware than at any other moment before in her life. She was sorry about the circumstances that had forced her to leave home. It had been wrong for her to have involved herself with the likes of Walton Springer.

Cephas Cross hesitated for a brief moment before he plunged into the cold waters of Nantucket Sound. He made a quick sign of the Cross before the waters closed over his head.

The trip from Savannah had been arduous, with danger at almost every turn. It had been on a poorly built ship, poorly maintained, with tattered sails that could not hold the wind. They'd had only spoiled, rotten, wormy meat to eat, and only rancid water to drink; along with a cruel and hateful captain, they had all helped Cephas in his decision to jump ship.

The ship was loaded with cotton bound for New England. Cephas had been on second watch when he'd realized that the shoreline had appeared like a gray mass on the horizon. He had looked about. The first mate, a true replica of the captain, had been at the wheel. Had he noticed the shoreline? Cephas had figured that at last his opportunity to leave had finally come. The man at the wheel had his back to Cephas.

Suddenly the first mate had turned and summoned him. Startled, his thoughts on escaping, Cephas had hurried to the man's side.

"Aye, sir. What is it, sir?" Oh, God, don't let it be that he has seen the shoreline.

"What is it, you frog-swallerin' bastard? What is it? Some hot grog from the galley, mate! 'Tis a friggin' cold night! Me hands are near froze to the wheel! On the double, ye bloody bastard!" the man spat after Cephas.

Cephas had scurried from the quarterdeck to the main deck below. But he did not continue to the galley on the lower deck. Instead, he had scrambled crablike, moving in the dark as silently and as quickly as he could on the slimy deck until he'd reached the poop deck. He had climbed to the top rail and dived silently into the cold, dark water. The first mate would wait a long time for his grog.

Since his early years, Cephas had been at home on the waterfront of Savannah. He had learned how to swim underwater, could hold his breath and speed like a slender fish. He was strong and determined.

Sally Lehigh usually walked her dog every morning. This particular morning, the dog's barking alerted her. That was when she saw a man's body, lying facedown in the sand. The body twitched suddenly as the dog ran back and forth, tossing sand into the air with his boisterous activity. The man spoke, his voice hoarse, the words barely intelligible. Sally Lehigh ran for help.

Cephas was happy with the pleasurable life he had discovered living near the ocean. His small skiff idled lazily against the shore. The bluefish had been running well, in large schools, in the coastal waters of the sound, and he had brought in a large catch. He would sell enough to get money for the new bed and mattress he had promised his young wife Sally. He knew what she would say. "Ah, Cephas, you spoil me with your wonderful gifts!"

He would smile back at her, reach for her long black hair to caress it lovingly, and tell her, "You are my heart, Sally. Never did I, a poor slave, expect that such a treasure waited for me up here in freedom land."

When Samuel was born, their happiness was complete. From his father, Sam had received a love for the sea and for new adventure, and strength to face the unknown. These were an inherent part of his life.

From his mother, who was part Indian, Samuel learned how to read the sky, the trees, the earth, and its secrets. He learned to read people as well. "Remember," his mother would say to him, "not everyone who smiles at you will be your friend. You may think there is honey in his heart, but it may be sour vinegar. And, my son," she would say, as she oiled his limbs for strength, "the eyes will speak, even while the tongue keeps silent." And finally, there was the truth that Samuel Cross kept close to his heart. "God gave you life; what you do with that gift should always honor the one who gave it."

Sam was thirteen when he signed on to a packet ship bound from Nantucket to England.

"Thou art a smart lad, Sam," the ship's crewmaster, a Quaker, told him. "Thou learnest well, taking thy lessons to heart. Thou knowest what is important; the merchant that owns this ship will be pleased with my report of such a willing worker."

"Thank you, sir," young Sam answered, "I try to do my best."

"Aye, and for Quakers such as we, it makes no difference about a man's color. Do good work, Sam, and thou shalt make the grade."

"Aye, sir." Sam was eager to please.

By the time he was nineteen, Sam Cross had reached the status of second mate. Now he was twenty and making his second trip to Canton, China, as first mate on the *Eastern Queen*.

Eight

Sam Cross's skin prickled with concern. He became aware that Zevia Sinclair had turned away from the ship's rail and was giving him her full attention.

His immediate response was to look directly at Zevia. He saw soft, melting skin the color of a sun-ripened peach, skin flawlessly smooth. Her eyes, looking back at him without the slightest caution, were wide, deep-set, black as ebony, framed by high sculpted cheekbones. Thick, black, luxurious curls peeked from beneath her bonnet.

She gave him only a hint of a smile, acknowledging that she had been studying him. She extended her gloved hand.

"First mate Cross, is it, sir?"

Her voice was low and unhurried, seemed to him almost as if she was speaking to a servant. Sam's eyebrows shot up in surprise. It was not what she had said, but the way she had said it. Who was she to find him lacking? he wondered. He answered quickly to dispel any misconceptions the girl might have.

"As first mate," he explained patiently, "I am second-in-command. I am responsible for the ship, its cargo, crew, and passengers," he emphasized, "when the captain is not aboard or is unable to take charge."

His eyes never left her face. He told himself that he was very happy that their paths would seldom cross. He would have enough to do to help sail the *Eastern Queen* to Canton and return to home port safely without concerning himself with Zevia Sinclair.

Sam Cross usually had little time for females. He had been at sea since he was thirteen. From cabin boy to cook's helper to carpenter's helper to seaman, he had sailed, he had learned, and he had developed his skills. He hoped to have his own ship under his command before he reached his twenty-second birthday. To do that meant there was little time for women in his life.

Captain Loring had been an exemplary teacher. He'd once told Sam, "Always know the crew—each man's strengths, weaknesses, and loyalties. If you find a bad one aboard, get rid of him quickly or confine him to the brig until you can. A rebel will sicken the rest of the crew like an evil disease. Be firm, but be fair. Remember, everyone's welfare on board depends on each man's willingness and ability to do his assigned task and do it right!"

Sam nodded thoughtfully. He understood the captain. He knew Captain Loring had given him the job of first mate because of Sam's knowledge of seamanship and his innate ability to work with all types of men from varying backgrounds.

The crew had been together for several voyages. They knew they were among the best paid, with a pint of grog every third day, good food, and clean berths. They were aware, also, that after three years on an American ship, they could be admitted to American citizenship. So there were Norwegians, Swedes, English, French, some Germans, and a few from Canada, signed on for the entire voyage.

Captain Loring and his first mate routinely met before sailing. This day, the captain sat at his desk in his private quarters and indicated to Sam the various bills of lading for the goods he was taking to Canton.

"We have fifty thousand silver dollars, several tons of lead, iron, quicksilver, as well as steel, brimstone, and copper. Our holds are nearly full. I hope I have enough space to load on some sea otter, beaver, and fox skins when we reach the northwest. The fur trade does well in China. The Mandarins love their sealskin and fur capes. All told, we have five million dollars worth of cargo. I hope to make a good profit of at least three million."

"I know, sir," Sam agreed. He was quiet for a moment. "Sir," he asked, "how many passengers are there?"

"Besides Miss Sinclair and my daughter, Jane, we have a Doctor Fitch and his wife, Mrs. Ellen Fitch, a German missionary priest, Father Fleishman, and a young merchant from Boston eager to visit the Orient. His name is Charles Morton. Six in all."

"Good. That should not be any problem. Are any of them infirm, in need of special care?"

"I wouldn't let them board if they were. You know that, Sam. The only one will be my daughter, and . . ."

"Oh, we'll take good care of her!" Sam answered quickly.

"Now, Sam," the captain indicated the documents on his desk, "these important papers concerning our cargo will always be locked in my sea chest." He pointed to a strongbox into which he placed the papers. Then he locked it with a key and proceeded toward his sleeping berth. He opened a sliding panel beneath the berth to reveal a large space, almost large enough to conceal a body, Sam thought.

"Only you, as second-in-command, know about this. And the key is on my keychain, which is always on my person. These papers are as valuable as currency."

"Indeed . . . I understand, Captain."

"So," Captain Loring said, "business concluded, let us have our customary drink." He pulled open a lower drawer of his desk and removed a bottle of brandy and two glasses. "How about a quick toast to the *Eastern Queen* and a successful voyage?" He raised his filled glass.

"Success and safe harbor," Sam answered.

"By the way," Captain Loring said, after he had taken several sips, "what do you think of Miss Sinclair, now that you've met her?"

Sam answered slowly. "She is very attractive, strong-willed, accustomed to having her way and . . . has been spoiled by a doting father."

"And her father?"

"Well, he's an interesting man. Seemed strange to me, couldn't figure out . . . a colored man with such a foreign accent . . . and foreign manners. Didn't seem American, somehow."

Captain Loring nodded. "I know what you mean. When I checked his daughter's references, found out he was reared in Germany. That accounts for some of it, I guess."

"Could be. Well, Captain, sir, here's to a profitable voyage," Sam said.

"To the *Eastern Queen!*" Captain Loring responded. His eyes took a measure of his first mate and he was satisfied with what he saw. Sam Cross would do the job, he'd bet his life on him. Here was a young man with the vigorous strains of a strong heritage that gave him determination to succeed, strong self-confidence, and a willingness to face odds without being ruthless or heartless. He was a good man, the best for the job, and the captain was happy to have him.

Zevia stood against the rail, watched the land mass disappear over the horizon as the *Eastern Queen* sailed on the evening tide.

Sandy Hook was the last she saw of land, and by then the ship had turned to sail blithely over the open ocean.

The mainsails had been partly unfurled and the ship had reached a moderate speed. There were seamen everywhere, pulling at ropes in unison, tightening the rigging lines and scrambling up and down the masts like energetic monkeys. The frenetic activity fascinated Zevia. Shouts and calls bombarded her ears as the work progressed and the ship made headway. From deep within, she heard the ship come alive. There were sounds of movement, groans, squeaks, and rumbles as the ship moved majestically to answer the call of a faraway port.

Zevia's thoughts turned to her father. True to his stoic nature, he made a goodbye that was brief and formal.

"Zevia," her father had said, "you are my daughter, and because you are, I know how you feel. Go, have your adventure, and return safe to me." He started to leave, then turned to her. *"Ach,* Miffy, I love you."

Following her father's cue, Zevia spoke quickly, in the same tone of voice, as if they were parting for only an hour.

"Papa, you know I love you, too."

After a brief hug, her father's dark coated figure hurried down the gangplank.

As she stood at the rail, remembering, sudden, unexpected tears pricked under her eyelids. She shook her head to flick them away. A man's voice behind her intruded into her thoughts.

"Not a good idea to stand about whenever the ship's crew is working. Better to stay below until things are well under way."

Zevia whirled about to see Sam Cross standing behind her. He was directing her to the companionway that led to the lower deck. His face was flushed, and Zevia could see an uncompromising grimness there. So as much as she wanted to protest, she thought better of it.

Without a word, she turned and made her way to her quarters. There would be time to deal with Sam Cross, first mate, later—she was sure of that. She remembered with bitterness her failed relationship with Walton Springer, the young man she thought she loved, in Boston, when she had studied there.

So Sam Cross needn't think she'd be a problem to him or to any of his crew. Men were not to be trusted, and it was just as well that she was aware of that fact. Sudden nausea pricked at her stomach. She was probably going to be seasick. Perhaps it was just as well to go below.

Zevia, irritated and stung by Sam's highhanded attitude, went to the small cabin that was to be her home for the next six months. She had a comfortable berth attached to the bulkhead, accommodating a lower storage space for articles of clothing. A small table and equally tiny chair were against the opposite wall, with a storage locker built into the wall. The space was so small that when she was in her berth she could stretch out her arms and almost reach the table. But it was a neat, compact space that met her need for tidiness. She had unpacked her trunk and put her clothing away, and the empty trunk had been stored away in some hold below deck.

She decided to dress for dinner; on the first night at sea, she guessed it would be expected. She would also meet the other passengers.

She had already met her charge, young Jane Loring, an appealing, dark-haired seven-year-old. Zevia knew what it was like to grow up without a mother. She empathized with the youngster. They became friends almost instantly.

"Zevia? Never heard that name before," Jane said, when told she could call her teacher Miss Zevia.

"It is a different name, isn't it? My mother gave it to me when I was born. But why don't you call me Miss Miffy, then? That's what my father calls me. Someday I'll tell you why," Zevia added.

"I like Miss Miffy," Jane had agreed, delighted by the friendliness Zevia showed her.

Dinner that night was a pleasant affair. There was a large dining salon amidship on the second deck. Like all Worrell Brothers' ships, the room had a Boston Brahmin quality in its decor. Furnished with a heavy oak table and chairs, and a huge candelabrum overhead, it appeared much like a room in the finest house on Beacon Hill. Oriental rugs, crystal sconces on the walls covered with rose silk damask, and a small woodburning fireplace made Zevia feel she was on land, except for the gentle rocking motion of the ship under her feet. A huge sideboard with a brass rail around its edge to keep plates from sliding with the ship's movement was decorated with an ornate carved mirror over it. The inner wall of the room protected a beautiful piano. Zevia was surprised and happy to see it. She loved music, a gift inherited from her father. She hoped the captain would allow her to play the instrument from time to time. She had not expected this added bonus. She could find comfort at the piano.

They were seated by the captain. He sat at the head and said to the missionary-priest, "Father Fleishman, it's only fitting that you sit at the other end, please. You will give the blessing, sir?"

Father Fleishman agreed, and after making the sign of the Cross, which the Catholics at the table followed, a blessing was said.

Jane was at her father's right and Sam Cross, as first mate, was on his left. Zevia was directed by the captain to sit next to Jane. The doctor's wife, Mrs. Fitch, was seated to Zevia's right. Dr. Fitch, a round-faced friendly man, was seated across from his wife, who seemed somewhat aloof to Zevia. She directed most of her conversation either to her husband or the priest. Charles Morton, a young Boston merchant being sent by his family to observe the Chinese market, had been seated across from Zevia.

The captain's cook proved that he knew his craft. A delicious light soup was served first, followed by a cold fish salad, delicately seasoned. The main course was roast chicken, accompanied by seasoned vegetables and dressing. Beautifully soft white rolls, freshly baked, appeared on the table with golden mounds of butter. Zevia ate with relish. Her nausea subsided.

"Glad to know you are seaworthy, Miss Sinclair," Captain Loring remarked. "You've had no problem with our voyage so far?" he asked.

"No, sir, I am doing well. It must be the sea air. I don't know when I've enjoyed food more. Your cook . . ."

"Knows what he's doing. He and his wife, Dorcas, have been with me on, say, what's this, our fourth voyage, eh, Dorcas?"

"That's right, Captain, sir," Dorcas, the Negro woman, said, as she deftly removed dishes to replace them with the next course.

Zevia was aware that Sam Cross had been silently observing her. He was attractive, his bronze skin reflected good health and vigor, and Zevia noticed his hands especially. They were long, with slender, tapered fingers. Nonetheless, she could see quiet strength in them as she watched him eat. He wore immaculate whites with a masculine dignity. She could tell by intuition that he was a proud man. His black hair curled around his ears, and she could see that his dark ebony eyes missed little.

Dr. Fitch spoke up.

"Mr. Cross, have you been to China before, too? What can we expect on this trip?"

Sam was somewhat startled by the doctor's inquiry. Most often people asked the captain questions like that one. He'd been so busy thinking about Zevia Sinclair, he almost did not hear the question. A single woman on board his ship—nothing but ill could come of it. Why would a young woman want to go so far from home? Another example of how spoiled she was—to wheedle her father into letting her do what she wanted. Well, Sam thought, she'll get no special treatment from me. He'd do his job, face up to his responsibilities, but the young lady needn't expect more attention from him. Besides, he didn't want to worry over her welfare. She chose to come, she'd be on her own.

Sam swallowed a sip of his wine and directed his attention to the doctor seated across the table from him.

"Perhaps, Dr. Fitch, you should ask our captain what to expect. But I can tell you, this will be a voyage you will remember. Every trip is different, and we expect to make stops along the way, and you'll see different countries, people . . ."

The captain broke in, "Sam is right, Dr. Fitch. But I must tell you, your wife will not go into China with you . . ."

"And why not, Captain?" Mrs. Fitch asked quickly, irritation evident on her face.

"Canton is the only port in China where we can enter and trade. Foreign women are not allowed in Canton. The Chinese see them as *guailo,* woman, *foreign devil."*

"Why, that's frightful! What will I do?" Mrs. Fitch exclaimed.

"Well," the captain said, "it will be up to you. While your husband may go into Canton 'factories,' none of us Americans can go further. So you can either remain aboard ship, or we can drop you off in Macao, to await our return. But, not to worry," he added kindly, "it'll be some time before you must make that decision."

Zevia wondered what all this would mean to her. The captain was still speaking.

"Chinese law says, 'Neither women, guns, spears, nor arms of any kind may be brought to factories.' Seems strange that they lump women and arms together as forbidden, doesn't it?" He smiled at Mrs. Fitch.

"What factory? I didn't think they manufactured goods," Charles Morton asked.

"Oh, no," Captain Loring explained quickly. " 'Factories' comes from the word 'factors,' the only brokers in Canton we can deal with. They are brokers appointed by the government. There is a small quarter-square-mile of land in Canton Harbor, Whang-po, where the factors do their business. So far, foreigners have not been allowed to venture past that area."

"Were you aware of this, Oliver?" Ellen Fitch queried her husband impatiently. "Did the university indicate such a thing to you?" Everyone at the table saw the angry dismay on her face.

The captain broke in, "The university may not have been aware, Mrs. Fitch. We haven't been trading with China that long. We'll take you to China . . . but you will see it only from the harbor. Sorry, but my daughter and Miss Sinclair are forbidden to enter as well. I plan to situate them in a private bungalow that I lease in Macao, an island near the harbor. It's a delightful place with beautiful grounds. There is a very efficient staff there, so you'd be welcome if you cared to stay there, too."

No one could miss Ellen Fitch's disappointment and her dismay at being relegated to some Portuguese colony with a child and her colored governess.

The meal came to a silent end, each person seemingly focused on his or her own personal future.

After coffee had been served, the captain turned to Zevia.

"Miss Sinclair, I know you have studied the piano. Would you mind playing something for us?"

"I'd be happy to, Captain Loring."

The men rose from their chairs as Zevia went to the piano. She turned the stool to a comfortable height and began to play. The music that flowed from beneath her fingers was of an almost professional quality. Zevia was grateful to her father for making her practice her piano. Often, he had told her, "There will be no regrets for doing a task well, Miffy. Practice, *Liebchen,* practice." So she played Chopin, Bach, and a Beethoven sonata to applause that she accepted with a gracious bow. She avoided looking at Sam, but she couldn't help but wonder what he really thought of her now.

Charles Morton spoke of her talent the next morning at breakfast.

"Where did you learn to play like that, Miss Sinclair?"

"In Maine, there's not much else to do."

"Well, it was mighty excellent," he said. "First class."

She hadn't wanted to, but she looked at Sam to see his reaction to the remark.

"Mighty fine," was all he said, as he continued to eat his breakfast.

Nine

The *Eastern Queen* moved steadily, making excellent travel time of almost two hundred miles a day, and it wasn't long before Zevia saw the brilliant blue-green waters of the Caribbean. Its beauty delighted her.

She couldn't help but notice the difference from the ocean around her native Maine. There was such a contrast to the angry waters that pounded the rocky shores of her home. The calm, placid Caribbean, its peacock-blue waters, flecked with an occasional crest of white sea foam, eased the tension Zevia felt. Perhaps, she thought, the tranquility of this ocean means peace in my life. Reluctant to leave the ship's rail where she stood, she sighed, straightened her shoulders, and went below to assume her duties to her young charge.

She had established a daily routine. Mornings were spent in the dining salon with Jane and her lessons. After Zevia's informal concert, Captain Loring asked her to give his daughter piano lessons. A half-hour after lunch was reserved for that activity. After that, Jane either took a nap or spent some part of the afternoon with her father. Zevia's obligations to Jane were complete by mid-afternoon.

* * *

Quite often by late afternoon she'd walk up to the top deck for fresh air, and to watch the many and varied activities needed to navigate the *Eastern Queen.* The crew was always cleaning, polishing, painting, recoiling ropes, checking the davits of the anchor and other equipment. The *Eastern Queen* was a beautiful ship. Zevia knew she was falling in love with her and felt a vicarious thrill knowing that it was her father's skill and ability as a draftsman that had brought the ship into being. Proud of her father, she wondered if anyone knew her father had designed the ship.

The ship's masts were tall and stalwart. Her sails were crisp and clean, strong enough to grasp the slightest wind and run with it. Although trim, neat, and ladylike, she was nevertheless strong enough to do the task she was built to do.

For some time Zevia stood and watched the waves roll and foam under the prow. She clutched her cloak close because of the strong wind. Suddenly she felt dizzy and queasy. Panic and fear overcame her. She struggled to maintain her balance, gulped to fill her lungs with air. Perhaps it came from watching the writhing, foaming waves roil beneath the prow as the ship's bowsprit dipped to taste the water. Zevia put her hand to her forehead, closed her eyes, and grabbed the ship's rail with her other hand to steady herself.

"Miss Sinclair."

Zevia wheeled about to see Sam Cross observing her, a deep scowl on his face.

"Maybe you ought not stand about."

"Stand about?" Zevia repeated. "What do you mean, 'Stand about'? I'm not allowed to be here?" she sputtered.

Sam gave a crooked grin as he noticed her pallor and unsteadiness.

As brash and as brave as Miss Zevia Sinclair tried to act, she was not the hardy sailor she would have everyone believe. Sam Cross had been at sea too long not to recognize physical distress. However, he thought he'd be prudent in his comments.

So he explained, "Captain Loring and I don't allow bad language from the men, but when they are busy workin', they sometimes let go with a swear or two, 'specially in bad weather."

Sam's dark eyes never left Zevia's face, and she was angry with herself for suddenly feeling intimidated by his authoritative voice. A black curl of his hair had fallen over his forehead. He brushed it from his eyes brusquely, as if annoyed by the distraction. Zevia noticed his long legs as he stood, black booted, both hands on his hips, waiting for her response. She saw, too, the large knife and pistol tucked into his waistband. She grasped her cloak tighter around her neck and shook her head.

"You needn't worry 'bout my ears, Mr. Cross. If you want me to go below, just say so. I don't want to be a distraction to you . . . or your men."

She saw angry glints in Sam's eyes and she heard the exasperation in his voice.

"Miss Sinclair, stay topside, by all means. But don't hold me responsible for what you see or hear. And I might as well tell you, a storm is headed our way."

"Not today; it's too beautiful," she protested. "Anyway, how do you know?"

"It's my business to know. Mark my words. Tomorrow at this time, you'll be glad to be below, and to *stay* there."

He touched his fingers to his head in a quick salute and turned on his heel, leaving Zevia standing alone.

Her face flushed with anger. Her nausea had left as suddenly as it had appeared. How dared he make predictions as to how she would feel? She heard him bellow orders to a seaman who'd scrambled hurriedly to do the first mate's bidding. He should pay heed to his own work, not me, she mused. It wasn't her fault, she thought, that she had been compelled to take this far-flung odyssey. Plague take Sam Cross!

Slowly, she made her way across the deck, around the coils of ropes, pails, buckets, and nautical gear she didn't know the names of or the uses for, and she was surprised to find herself happy to get to her quarters.

Her legs were weak and trembling, and she experienced a cramping sensation in her lower abdomen. Never should have eaten that rich fruit cake that Dorcas had served at dinner last night. She poured some water from the carafe on her bedside table, took a few sips before she rested on her berth. She'd feel better before dinner, she was certain.

Dinner was unpleasant. Dishes slid about the table, and even though heavy-bottomed mugs had been used instead of glassware, each diner's appetite was affected.

Mrs. Fitch was paler and more taciturn than ever. Her husband tried to reassure her, but her discomfort only increased.

"Come, Ellen, I'll take you back to our cabin," her husband suggested. The couple excused themselves and left, staggering like a pair of inebriates as they made their way. Zevia finished her soup and then she, too, asked to be excused.

The captain spoke to her.

"Miss Sinclair, you will find straps along the sides of your berth. Strap yourself in so's you won't be pitched out," Captain Loring advised. "Don't expect this storm to get much worse," he tried to reassure her. "The glass is holding steady."

As she passed by Dorcas at the serving board, the woman whispered, "Bring you something later, Miss Zevia."

Zevia nodded numbly and tried to match her steps with the turbulent movements of the tossing ship. It was difficult.

By midnight that night, the storm struck in a vigorous fury. Northern winds threatened to push the ship off course. Captain Loring and Sam Cross were both at the wheel.

"Order close-reefed sails!" the captain shouted to his first mate.

"Done, sir," Sam replied. "The crew have shorten'd the mains'ls and hauled to . . . we'd best . . ."

The words never left Sam's mouth. They were silenced by a booming rumble of thunder, followed by a jagged flash of lightning. The ship's mainmast was struck. The topspar and top mainsail tore away with a keening cry and hung awkwardly as the crew quickly rushed to repair the damage.

"Cut the riggin', man!" Shouts came from Harry Traxton, bosun's mate, as he tried to direct his men. He was everywhere, his yellow slicker flashed in the dark rain as he sought to save the ship. He was in charge of the ship's deck crew. His sharp whistle, accompanied by his orders, brought some order to the chaos of the stricken ship.

The rain fell in thick sheets, visibility was almost impossible, and the wind whipped the loose riggings into angry lashes as the crew tried to carry out his orders.

A second fiery bolt cracked and split the mizzenmast like a fragile twig. Two crewmen who had been trying to reef the topsails were flung to the deck below and were pinned to the slippery surface by heavy, sodden sails.

"Heave to! Get 'em out!" the bosun directed, as they rushed to the stricken men. The storm screamed and railed about them. Confusion reigned.

At the wheel, Captain Loring and Sam studied the compass. Affected by lightning, its needle spun wildly.

"Sam," the captain worried, "hold her steady. We may lose our course."

"Aye, sir," Sam gasped. "Steady as she goes."

"Got to hold 'er, Sam. I'm going aft to check the damage."

The captain was dismayed when he saw the wreckage. The top gallants on the mainmast and broken mizzenmast were gone. The other sails had been partially reefed, but not too close, so there were shredded, torn sheets of sail flapping erratically, blowing as if trying desperately to purchase some viable wind.

He saw Dr. Fitch tending to the injured men.

"How bad is it, Doctor?"

"A fractured leg on one, and a possible concussion on the other; he took a severe blow to the head. Sending them below for now," the doctor said.

"Good work. Thanks, Doctor."

Then the captain shouted.

"Every hand, heave to." To Harry Traxton, he shouted, "Get the carpenters up here on the double, clear away the wreckage! Save what you can. Chuck the rest."

"Aye, sir. Will do, sir," the bosun said.

"Good man, Harry. Counting on you to get this ship in good order. There'll be a double portion of grog for every man when this is over."

"Aye, sir!" Harry agreed quickly.

The captain wondered. They were less than one-quarter of the journey along. Was the storm an omen?

Night and day the crew worked to repair the ship. The sailmaker's gang made and fitted new sails, the carpenters that were always on board ship to handle such work made new masts, and some of the stumps of the top masts were saved.

Dorcas and Josiah, for their part, saw that there was plenty of food. Pots of hot coffee were always ready, and sandwiches made of thick slabs of fresh bread and meat, plus bowls of hearty stew. There was always a hungry sailor needing sustenance. The passengers, too, were kept appeased and comforted by the excellent meals presented to them.

Whenever Dorcas could spare a moment from her galley duties, she checked on Zevia, who remained quiet and frightened, wrapped in blankets on her berth.

"I see the bleedin's stopped," Dorcas told the worried girl, when she completed her examination. "You'll be all right. Just like this here storm is over, an' we're sailin' out of the worst, your own storm is past. Put it behind you . . ."

"How can I, Dorcas? I feel so . . ."

" 'Course you can! Don't be cryin' over what's past! Like I said, since Eve had that problem with that snake—

well, you know, you live and learn. Here," she pulled Zevia to a sitting position and arranged a small tray on her lap. "Brought you some hot soup."

"Dorcas, has anyone asked . . ." Zevia queried.

"Uh-huh, too busy gettin' things ready to sail. Most of the others keepin' to their cabins, too. Think we'll be sailin' soon, far's I can see. Repairs most all done, Josiah said the men told him."

Within a few days, it was as if the storm had never happened. Soon the *Eastern Queen* was under sail.

Sam Cross discovered, however, that the compass needle was off by five points and that sure enough, they were east of their planned course. He took a bearing from the sun and the North Star and endeavored to get back on course.

"Sam," Captain Loring suggested, "get me a ten-foot board. I believe the compass has been magnetized by the lightning and the iron we have in the hold. Let's try this."

He placed the compass at the end of the ten-foot board, tied it securely, and extended it out from the side of the ship. The compass corrected itself and the true course was discovered.

Sam Cross knew he would never forget that lesson. Captain Loring was a good man to learn from.

The dreadful storm that had been endured by all seemed to bring the passengers closer together.

Mrs. Fitch appeared to take a motherly interest in little Jane and had started the child on some needlework. Charles Morton spent a good deal of his time with Captain Loring, asking questions about the China trade. Dr. Fitch made himself available to tend to the medical problems of the crew and monitored the recovery of those who had been injured.

Captain Loring spoke to the priest.

"Father, I must ask you, if you could, would you remove your clerical collar?"

"Remove my collar? Why should I do such a thing? I am a priest and should be recognized as a priest." The man's face flushed with indignation.

"Oh, Father, I understand," Captain Loring said. "However, I am certain you know that many superstitions abound among seafaring men. One of them is that a priest brings bad luck to a ship. They often connect a priest with death. So, if you don't mind . . ."

"Of course I mind, Captain, but I see the wisdom of maintaining peace on your ship. I will remove the collar."

Dieter Fleishman was a slender young man but nonetheless seemed to be quite strong, like someone who paid attention to his body. He walked the deck daily and paid rigorous attention to his diet. Spartan when it came to Dorcas's rich desserts, he loved her rolls. Whenever the German reached across the table for one of Dorcas's plump, fluffy rolls, Sam noticed the unusual amount of thick reddish hair that covered the backs of his hands and forearms. The coarse appearance remained in Sam's mind.

Sam had been so busy with the storm and its aftermath that he missed many dinner meals, taking most at the wheel or whenever he could. Zevia missed meals as well. Everyone assumed it was the storm that had caused her to be absent, and Dorcas implied that indeed the weather "had upset Miss Zevia."

"But you're making sure she's taken care of, aren't you, Dorcas?" the captain asked.

"Yes, sir, makin' sure. She'll be fine in a day or so."

"If I can be of help . . ." Dr. Fitch offered. "Maybe have a look . . ."

"No, sir, not right now. She just a bit under the weather, sir," Dorcas insisted.

When Dorcas checked Zevia later that evening, she encouraged her to resume her duties.

"Best you move from this berth. Brought you some hot beef broth . . . good for gettin' your strength back. I told the captain that you under the weather due to the storm. Been two days now, everythin's calm, and you be better out of this cubbyhole."

That night at dinner, both Sam and Zevia were at the table. Sam paid special attention to Zevia. Her skin had lost its peachlike bloom, and her eyes were like deep pools of sorrow. He asked her how she was feeling. Zevia smiled weakly.

"I'm doing nicely. You were right about the storm, and yes," she nodded her head, "I *was* glad to stay below."

"We all were," Charles Morton said. "Will there be more storms, Captain?"

"The sea is like a woman, Mr. Morton," Captain Loring said, as he drained his wineglass and motioned for Dorcas to refill it. "She may change from one day to the next, but that's what makes her so fascinating." He added seriously, "We do our best to avoid storms, but Mother Nature sometimes tricks us and we have to live with whatever she sends."

An involuntary shiver traveled up Zevia's spine when she heard the captain's words "Mother Nature tricks us . . . we have to live with it."

Could anyone tell by looking at her that her own innocence, her virginity, was gone, lost forever? She had
all she could do to control her emotions. She wanted to
wail aloud, scream and moan over the grievous, unjust
situation through which she had suffered. Damn that
Walton. Instead of lasting happiness, trusting and believing him had brought only self-loathing and misery. How
would she ever live with what had happened to her? She
felt soiled, stained, damaged. How could she face Oma,
her grandmother, or her father? How could she live with
this awful secret? Sam Cross was speaking to her. She
raised her head to listen to him.

"Miss Sinclair, would you like to go topside?"

She nodded wordlessly, suddenly determined to push
the past back—to force herself to fight for a future, this
time of her own choosing.

Sam pulled her chair back from the table as she excused herself.

"Certain I won't be . . . in the way?"

"Oh, no, Miss Sinclair," he apologized. "I'm afraid
I've been awful to you, always chasing you below deck.
But tonight it's mighty pleasant up on deck. Getting close
to the Equator. The sky's changing, the Southern Cross
is showing now."

As they moved up the companionway, he offered his
hand in a gesture of assistance, but Zevia ignored his
offered hand and made her own way.

Sam noticed but said nothing. He admired independence, and for some reason, he wanted to see the
warm glow in her cheeks again. She interested him, this
independent slip of a girl, as determined as he had been
not to let such a thing happen.

* * *

Dorcas had insisted, "Look, girl, you got to get on with your life. God gave you a healthy body and a good, sensible mind. I know . . ."

Zevia winced at Dorcas's words.

"I'll never get over what's happened to me," she complained.

The two women often shared a cup of tea at night after Dorcas's galley chores were completed. Zevia looked forward to the quiet visits with her supportive friend.

"Well, I won't, I just know it," Zevia continued. "My father and grandparents would be so ashamed . . ."

"Don't believe that, not for a minute," Dorcas broke in. "They love you, and that's all there is to it! I know if you were *my* child, I wouldn't stop loving you. Never! Besides, everybody's got secrets. You just don't know 'bout them, that's all."

"Everybody, Dorcas?"

"Everybody." Dorcas nodded. She laughed. "Even me got secrets my Josiah don't know nothin' about. Now, you hear me and hear me good. There's Sam Cross, the first mate on this ship. He's a good man if ever I saw one. Sailed with him before, an' I trust him, Josiah and me both."

"Dorcas, I don't want to be bothered with any more young men."

"Who said you had to be bothered? You know you got a long trip ahead of you, months and months. You're bound to be close together on this ship. So what I'm saying is, if Sam offers to be a friend to you, accept his friendship. It will make the trip easier, and help you get a grip on yourself. God knows you need to build up your confidence in yourself."

So Zevia surprised herself when she took Dorcas's advice and accepted Sam's invitation. Perhaps Dorcas was right: she needed to forget the past and get on with her life.

Ten

One evening, shortly after the storm, Charles Morton shared an after-dinner brandy and coffee with Captain Loring. The Fitches and Mr. Fleishman had declined to share in the after-dinner ritual and had gone to their separate quarters. Sam explained to the captain that he would like to teach Miss Sinclair how to navigate by the stars.

"Miss Sinclair is very quick, Captain, think you'll have another first-class navigator in your crew," Sam said with a grin.

The captain raised his eyebrows and smiled. "As you know, Sam, sometimes we need all the help we can get. So, please see that Miss Sinclair learns her lessons well." He dismissed the couple with a benediction-like wave of his hand.

" 'Tis my privilege, sir," Sam answered, as he led Zevia to the door. Zevia hesitated briefly, turned back to the captain to speak to him.

"How about Jane? Shouldn't I tuck her in for the night first, sir?"

"Oh, no, you go off with Sam. Dorcas is seeing to her tonight, and I plan to check her later."

"Well, then," Zevia said, "goodnight."

Charles Morton stared at the pair as they left. When

he turned his attention back to the captain, there was a wry expression on his face.

"I've noticed, Captain, the number of Negroes that you have on this ship. More than I had expected to see." He numbered them. "Your first mate, your daughter's governess, your cook, even several crewmen. All are colored people. Do you really trust these people and . . . their work?"

The captain didn't answer at first, and Charles noticed at once how quiet and thoughtful the captain became, as if reflecting on some personal history.

Charles looked at a man well over six feet tall, with a bigness about him due mainly to firm, hard muscles. He was always dressed in immaculate whites, his dark beard always neatly trimmed. He wore his rank of captain with confidence and authority. All of this was evident in his voice, his manner, and his direct gaze. Nothing about him was haphazard or frivolous. He was the personification of the captain of a clipper ship. He knew his ship, every inch of her, every man in his crew, and he had come to grips with his destiny.

"Do I understand that you are nineteen?" the captain asked.

"I just had a birthday, before coming on this trip. Taking a year off from Harvard. Be a senior when I return," Charles answered.

"Ummm. Good. You'll be well seasoned in the ways of the world after this trip."

He rose from his chair, went over to look out a porthole. Charles noticed a slight limp he hadn't observed before. Evidently satisfied with what he had seen, the captain returned to his seat, sat down, rubbed his right knee, a twinge of pain obviously reminding him of something.

"Charles, when I was nineteen, I had already been on several sea voyages. I discovered early, on the sea, a man or a woman's worth does not depend on skin color. I was a crewman and Sam was a cabin boy when we first met. We've both grown a lot since then. And I know that his goal is to captain his own ship one day. Can't think of a better man. I'd sail under him any day."

"Oh, it's not that I don't think he's capable . . ."

"What is it, then?"

Charles's face reddened when he realized that Captain Loring was somewhat irritated by his objections.

"I never knew that a colored man could think, could react, could be . . . trustworthy. Thought of them as . . ."

"Like slaves or chattel . . . people to be taken care of, you mean."

"Well, yes, I thought . . ."

"Got a lot to learn, son. Miss Sinclair and her folks have lived down Maine for years. I don't believe she'd like to know that you think of her as property. Don't know when I've met a more independent or proud young woman, or a better educated one. Sam Cross has never been a slave. His parents were free, and so is he. Father's a seaman from Savannah, and his mother is from a Nantucket family. Don't know what that makes him, except his own man. But to get back to your wondering why I trust him so, give him authority, so to speak."

"I *am* curious about that, sir."

"Well," the captain sipped his brandy with satisfaction, then continued with his story. "Some seasons back, on one of our first trips to the East, we had just come out of the doldrums near the Equator, coming into the South China Sea, when it happened."

"What happened, sir?"

"I got this bum knee. We were hoping for some trade winds to find us, been laid by for several days, we were all edgy and wanted to move. It was off the coast of Malaysia that we were attacked."

"Attacked?"

"Malaysian pirates. They had small boats with a single triangular sail and a small outrigger. What they did was, the bastards hid low in their crafts, with only one or two men showing until they were several hundred yards away from us. Then, as they got closer, they rose up, yelling, screaming the most unimaginable sounds I've ever heard. The lookout spotted them. Sam was at the wheel . . . 'course, we all heard them. See, they were tricky, because sometimes natives would come out from the islands with fresh fruits and vegetables to sell, but this time . . ."

"What did you do? How'd you get away?"

"Like I said, we'd had little winds for days, but I'd ordered the sheets unfurled just in case, and the ship was like a trembling racehorse, eager to be under way. We'd get an occasional gust or two, but that was all. So, when the pirates tried to board us, I called for all hands to 'hove to.' I've no man on any of my ships who can't fight. Most of the older ones been privateers themselves, anyway, so fighting's no problem. They're always ready. I'm sure you've noticed on the *Eastern Queen* we have guns at our gunports. That particular ship, the *Princess Royal,* had ten guns, eight four-pounders and two six-pounders."

The captain's eyes narrowed with memory as Charles waited for the rest of the story.

"We loaded with round shot and bags of musket balls and repelled the invaders. There must have been twenty or more of those boats coming at us. My men used knives, hatchets, and cutlasses to discourage any who climbed up like monkeys, trying to board. The noise, the confusion, the heat, and the immobility of my besieged ship stirred me to act. I ran shouting to Sam. We had to get out of this fix.

" 'Turn her to starboard, hard, hard!' I yelled. Sam saw me coming, heard me, and turned the wheel right quick. We had been scarcely moving, which is why the bastards got up to us so easily. Suddenly, I felt a sharp pain in my right leg and I fell. A bullet had struck me. Sam got a shot off at the bastard who shot me, got him in the throat, and with his other hand, turned the wheel opposite to port. The sudden swerve almost keeled over the *Princess Royal,* but the unexpected movement shook off the pirates trying to board. The gods were with us because the southeast trade winds that we had waited for so long came up. With the sails at the ready, we got out of there fast. So you see, I trust Sam Cross with my life. The sea is no place to be with untrustworthy companions. Color, nationality, race—none of that counts. It's the man and what's inside him that matters."

Charles nodded, aware that he had a great deal to learn, that so far, his life experiences had not prepared him for what was ahead.

The captain had still more information for Charles.

"Miss Sinclair's father is a ship designer. Did you know that?"

"No, sir, I didn't know."

"Neither did I until I took over this ship. The *Eastern Queen,* she's a Worrell-built ship, and when I took command, Angus Worrell showed me her brass nameplate near the bowsprit." He indicated it.

Eastern Queen, built by Worrell Brothers.
Designed by Alexander Sinclair.

"Well, I'll be damned," Charles Morton said.
"Thought you would be," the captain smiled.

Eleven

It was truly a night designed for lovers, Zevia thought, not mere acquaintances like her and Sam. The welcoming salt spray of the ocean cooled her flushed face as reluctantly she allowed herself to stand beside Sam on the upper deck.

The ocean was a sea of black, but the *Eastern Queen* clipped easily over white, frothy, breaking waves. Her bowsprit dipped delightedly toward the water, much like a courtesan requesting permission for a lady's hand. The moon, splendidly bright, was beautiful as it rode the black velvet sky. Brilliant diamond-like stars studded the heavens. Zevia felt emotionally stimulated by the extraordinary setting. She wondered what Sam would say if he knew how vulnerable she really was. She vowed silently that neither he nor any other man would ever know. She'd make her living as a governess, schoolteacher, whatever, but never would she be tricked by another man.

She was satisfied with the distraction of Sam's navigation lesson, but equally unhappy because despite herself, she had to acknowledge that he was an attractive man.

He was tall, with bronze, sun-burnished skin, and his eyes were dark, a deep brown that seemed to Zevia to be able to penetrate the heavens. She could tell by his enthusiasm that he was eager to share his knowledge of sea and sky with her.

Sam was explaining something to her. Concentrating, Zevia made herself listen. In her mind she found herself comparing Sam to Walton Springer. She could almost hear her former lover's smooth, silky voice, see his eyes, and feel his hands on her body.

"Zev, my dearest, there's never been anyone but you. If you leave me, there'll be no light in my life. I love you, only you," he had said, as his hands had flown like feathery wands over her tense, hungry young body. Hard as she tried, she could not will her body to resist his advances. Never before had she experienced such feelings.

She could now visualize her grandmother's serious face, her deep brown eyes peering beneath her ever-present head cloth, telling her for the thousandth time, "Remember, when you're away from home, be a lady, be sweet, remember your momma wanted the best for you." If she wanted the best for me, why did she die and leave me? Zevia had wanted to ask. Why didn't Oma tell her what to do in times like this? What would they say if they ever found out? Her father, with his ever-present Teutonic need to be perfect, and Oma, whose grief over her own loss would only be compounded by her granddaughter's transgression. Somehow, this awful secret would have to stay hidden from those who loved her. The secret would have to die with her. Only Dorcas knew. Zevia trusted her to keep silent.

Sam had positioned himself behind her, had extended his arm to point to a cluster of stars.

"See, Miss Sinclair, there's the Southern Cross, a constellation found only in the southern hemisphere."

"It is beautiful," Zevia breathed, as she tried to ignore the flush within her own body, caused, she knew, by Sam's nearness. She could feel his warm breath against her ear as he continued to tell her how important this constellation was to sailors.

God's breath, she swore to herself, my own body is turning against me! What's wrong with me? Am I turning into a loose woman? Where was the resolution she'd just vowed only moments before?

Dorcas had said to her, "Honey, be ready for your feelings to ride up and down, because you just been through a bad time. Keep your wits about you and think on what you want for yourself. Sometimes you might be scared, but no matter, hold your head high. Don't ever be 'shamed that you were weak once; be strong from now on. Always learn from your mistakes. That's what makes a strong woman."

Although it had been about a week since the miscarriage, Zevia felt weak and nervous. Would the feeling ever leave? Would she ever feel strong and sure of herself again?

She was pinned against the deck rail. Sam's left hand was on her shoulder as he continued to point with his right hand to show her Centaurus and Musca, the major stars of the Southern Cross. When he touched Zevia's shoulder, he was suddenly aware of the honesty of the moment. He *wanted* to touch her. To get past the excitement of the momentous revelation, he hurriedly continued to speak.

"Ever since I was a lad," he explained, "I've loved the sea. My father was a sailor from Savannah, and I guess there's more water in my body than there is blood. My dream is to have my own ship under my own command someday."

"My papa always told me that if you can dream of what you want, your dream can come true," Zevia said.

"I believe that, too, Miss Sinclair. This will be my second trip to the East with Captain Loring, and I hope that next time I make the trip, it will be as captain." He pressed his hand more firmly on her shoulder to steady her as the ship dipped to meet an oncoming wave. Zevia felt the warmth of his hand through her cape. She'd have to move to get away. He was too close. Perhaps now would be a good time to tell him what she had overheard.

Quickly, she bent her knees and slipped down so that she could move her head under his arm. She stepped aside and turned to face him. When she spoke, she tried to keep her voice calm and matter-of-fact. She pretended not to notice the surprised look on his face.

"Mr. Cross," she started.

"Sam, please, Miss Sinclair, Sam . . ."

"Well, then, Sam. And you may call me Zevia . . ."

"Only when we're alone," Sam interrupted. "Around the others, it will be Miss Sinclair. I will not tolerate disrespect from anybody—and in turn will not disrespect you," he insisted.

"Thank you, Sam. That's really nice of you. May I ask a question . . . about the ship?"

"Of course. What?" he frowned.

"Maybe you can't tell me, but do you have special papers for the goods and cargo you are taking to trade in China?"

"Why do you ask?" Sam frowned, surprised by her question.

"Perhaps you didn't know, Sam, but I speak and understand German. My father lived as an indentured servant in Germany for many years . . . grew up there, really. He was apprenticed to a draftsman, became a ship designer when he came back home. Did you know he designed the *Eastern Queen?*" she asked.

"Your father is Alexander Sinclair, the man who designed this ship?" Sam could hardly believe Zevia's words.

"Yes, he did. When he saw her in New York, he said he felt better about me leaving him, knowing I was on a ship he had designed."

"Well, I should say so!" Sam agreed.

"Anyway," Zevia continued, "last night, after dinner, when I was returning to my room, I heard Mr. Fleishman speak in German to one of the crew. Sounded to me as if he wanted to know about the ship's cargo, its value, and asked the crewman if he knew where the cargo's listing was kept. I heard the word *'Frachtbrief,'* consignment."

"Damn!" Sam exploded. "I was always suspicious of that priest. Had a difficult time saying grace the first night at sea. What did the other crewman look like?"

"Big, tall, with reddish hair and a beard. He spoke German, too."

"Hans Wolton. Signed on two years ago when the *Eastern Queen* was in Hamburg. Been a fine seaman. Up to now, that is."

Sam's face turned grim with the news she had given him. The navigation lesson was over.

Fleishman was glad he'd been asked to remove the clerical collar. The disguise had begun to chafe at him.

He had been ill prepared that first evening when Captain Loring had asked him to give the blessing over dinner. Thank God, he thought, he'd remembered a little Latin. He hoped no one had noticed his hesitation over the *Pater Noster.* He was so nervous, he couldn't remember anything else.

He recalled with grim memory his fruitless visit to his uncle's house.

"Now that you are fourteen, Dieter, you should apply to the *Hochschule,*" his mother told him. "I'm sure my brother Franz will keep his promise to help you with money. He has been in the military all his life, never married—so you are his only relative besides me."

Dieter's mother assured him that if they went to the city to visit her brother, he would be bound to help his nephew. Dieter could become a mechanical engineer—it was what he'd dreamed of being. He'd even brought some of his projects his teachers had said showed promise.

But there was no money.

"Money?" his uncle said. He looked at his sister, Dieter's mother. "You never came around before to see me, Hannah, so why now? Even when I had my war injury, you never came."

"But Franz, you said we shouldn't come!" his sister protested. "You told us you were all right and not to make the long trip! Besides," she reminded him, "you promised . . ."

"So now you make the long trip for nothing. My son here, Alexander, stayed by my side when I was recovering—I leave everything to him."

"Son! The *Schwartze* you call 'son'?" Hannah Fleishman said, disbelieving. "He is your servant!"

The old Hessian grunted and waved his hand. "Alexander is more son to me than you could ever know. There is nothing here for either of you."

Dieter Fleishman saw the look of love on his uncle's face directed at Alexander Sinclair. Bitterness toward the black servant rose in his throat. He had been denied by his own family for someone who was beneath him. His hatred for Alexander Sinclair knew no bounds.

Now his uncle was dead, the "son" doing well in America, he'd been told. It wasn't fair that a black man should be more successful than he. Dieter would make him pay, somehow. Bitter disappointment raged within him. The military life of his uncle that his mother suggested he try angered him even more.

"No, never," he told his mother. "I will not be a soldier like him. Never!"

Even though chaos reigned in central Europe, with governments dissenting and struggling, he would not wait to be called up. Instead, he almost ran to sign up on the first ship out of the city's harbor. It was a coal ship bound for Australia. For some obscure reason, the young lad felt a certain peace while at sea. He worked hard and quickly learned the skills he needed to be a good sailor.

On the dusty streets of Australia's harbors, he heard the news of gold in California. He turned his eyes to the New World.

He decided that his habit of disguising himself would work to his advantage. So it was as a missionary-priest that he paid his passage on the *Eastern Queen,* bound for China via San Francisco. Perhaps then he would yet find the good luck that had eluded him.

But good luck found him. He was on his way forward to the companionway of the middle deck when he collided with a stranger. The man he saw was a big red-haired German with a fiery red beard. Dieter could scarcely believe his eyes.

"Hans! Hans Wolton! What are you doing here? How long have you been on this ship?"

Neither man saw Zevia standing in the dark near the wheel. Fear and surprise clutched Zevia's heart as she heard the exchange.

"Dieter? By God, it is you! I've been on the ship since Hamburg. One of the crew. But what brings you here on the *Eastern Queen?* Oh, you're the one passenger the crew said was a priest?"

"Nein, sh, sh," Dieter admonished him, "just for now . . . I'm on my way to the gold fields in California."

"Think they need priests, Dieter?" Hans shook his head with laughter. "Not likely. Need men to handle shovel and pickax, more'n not." He slapped his cousin heartily on the back.

Hans stood beside his cousin, a slim, ascetic man who looked much the way he thought a priest should. But Hans noted, too, a hardness, a cruel twist to the younger man's mouth.

"Thought you were going to be an engineer, Dieter, not a seafaring man like me. Certainly not a priest."

Dieter shook his head. "Life changes, Hans, and one has to change with it. I needed money for school, thought my soldier-uncle would start me off, at least. Our family, you know, Hans, has always helped one another. Besides that, my uncle promised my mother when my father died, I was only ten years old, that he would help with my schooling. But no, he practically adopted the *Schwartze* that he had brought from America as an indentured servant. Now Alexander Sinclair is doing well as a ship designer. Even designed this ship, the *Eastern Queen.*"

"How do you know that?" Disbelief showed on his cousin's face.

"He was at the dock before we left. I heard the captain speak to him. It's his daughter that the captain has hired as his daughter's governess. I saw him. He did not see me. I was boarding the ship when I overheard the conversation."

"You saw Miss Sinclair? And her father?"

"The same," Dieter explained. "I heard him tell the captain that he felt better knowing that his daughter would be aboard a ship of his own design. I'd like to finish off both of them, father and daughter."

Zevia shivered in the dark as she heard the words and realized the ill will directed toward her and her father. She felt helpless.

Suddenly Hans's face brightened, as if he'd been struck by a great idea.

"Dieter! Listen, my cousin, you don't have to go for pickax and shovel! All you need is right here, on this ship!"

"What do you mean? The girl? Kidnap her?"

"No, damn, not the girl! Thousands of dollars right under your two feet, below deck. And I know how we can get it. All we need is the *Frachtbrief,* the consignment list, to present to the Chinese factors. We lock up the captain and first mate, pick up a 'chop,' a pass, to go up the Pearl River to Whampoa and trade with the Chinese. They know only the one who has the consignment list is the one to do business with. And we'll be the traders with the list and the pass. We don't even have to lift another finger. Find a ship that's leaving port, and we're on our way!"

Neither saw Zevia Sinclair, who was almost paralyzed by what she had heard.

Twelve

A few days later, the *Eastern Queen* rested at anchor near a small island off the coast of Chile. Captain Loring had wasted no time. As soon as Sam reported what Zevia had overheard, the captain ordered both men confined to the brig. When the anchor was finally dropped, the two miscreants were rowed to the island and left there. Strangely enough, neither claimed innocence. Sam realized, however, that as long as either of them lived, he would never forget the hatred he saw in the "priest's" eyes. He will be my enemy forever, Sam thought.

Sam was no stranger to enemies. There were those who did not like him, mainly because of his color. However, Sam wore his identity like a badge of honor. He was proud of his ancestry and did not care if others tried to diminish him because of who he was.

As he watched the coast of Chile recede in the distance, he remembered an incident that could have cost him his life. The ship he was sailing on, with cargo bound for the northwest, was rounding the Horn, moving from fifty degrees south latitude in the Atlantic to fifty degrees south latitude in the Pacific. The arctic cold had frozen the ropes into icy steel-like wires. Sleek sheets of water made progress on the decks precarious and treacherous. Sam had to claw his way, sometimes falling a few feet at a time, sometimes crawling along the slippery cold main topmast and studding sail boom to reach the sail. The shroud had to be released, as it was fouled up in the rigging.

A man was already aloft, trying vainly to grasp the halyard to lower the sail. The heavy wet sail slapped him back and forth with each icy buffet. When Sam finally reached the young tar, he swung the rope he had tied around his own waist to that of the sailor. In his fearful wild state, the sailor, his eyes widened with fright, grabbed Sam around the neck and held on with the ferocity of the doomed. Wind and rain slashed at their faces; their clothing, wet and icebound, weighted them down even more as layers of ice stiffened and hampered their movements. They were like robots encased in armor. The ship suddenly rolled disastrously.

"Leave go, man!" Sam shouted. "Leave go . . . we'll both . . ." he shouted, as he tried to pry the clawing fingers from his throat. The panic in the boy's face told Sam he had to act quickly if he was going to be able to save their lives.

Finally, in desperation, even though he knew all eyes below were on him, he struck the hysterical sailor a fierce blow to the side of his head. The ship quivered as it endeavored to meet the sudden variations of the wind. Sam and the sailor hung, swinging freely from the boom, held fast only by Sam's rope. When the ship rolled back, Sam was able to grasp the icy mast, release the rope with his almost numb fingers, and slide to safety, the unconscious sailor in his arms.

A relieved shout went up from the men watching on deck.

"Gor, man, sure 'n you took a godawful chance, by

damn." One of the sailors slapped Sam on the back, handed him a cup of grog, then threw a blanket over his shoulders. Sam mumbled his thanks as he stumbled below for warm, dry clothing.

Later that evening, after the storm had passed, they were moving into calmer waters and each man clasped his fists around his welcome cup of evening grog. The bosun's mate, a hardened sailor from Liverpool who had made no bones about his dislike for Sam—"never wanted to work wid a cullud bloke," he'd said—stood up and demanded everyone's attention. Flecks of foam and spittle flew from the man's mouth as he spoke.

"Now, see 'ere, ye hardhearted, lecherous bastards. Ye kno' I'm a man wot speaks me mind, good or bad! Faith, now 'tis time fer me ter swally me 'ateful thoughts 'n ter praise one decent 'uman bein' among us 'ere that's not o' our color, but by God, is a man by any measure!" He raised his cup, pointed it in Sam's direction.

"To Sam Cross, the best black or white man I've ever 'ad the luck ter be sailin' with! Sam Cross!" he shouted.

" 'Ear, 'ear," the cries echoed from the men as they slapped their mugs on the table. They quieted down when Sam rose to speak. He was sixteen years old. He'd always remembered his father's words, "To be treated like a man, you have to act like a man." He raised his hand in acknowledgment of their good wishes.

He spoke quietly.

"I only did what any decent man would do. Hope you'd do the same for me."

Now, years later, Sam remembered the incident. There had been many more such incidents, causing him to be constantly tested and tried by his peers. In this world of seafaring and trade, he knew it would always be so. He prayed that he could meet the challenge. He put the images of Dieter Fleishman and Hans Wolton in the back of his mind. The business at hand now was to reach Macao, settle the women in Captain Loring's compound, and then go on to Canton. The southeast trade winds would be bearing down on them—they could expect to make progress.

Sam's thoughts turned to Zevia. How was she doing? Since the night she had given him the news about the criminal intent of Dieter and Hans, he had been so busy with their disposition he had hardly seen her. Indeed, Captain Loring had explained to the passengers that the "priest" had asked to be put ashore—a change in his plans, he said. "Wanted to minister to the uncivilized Indians," the captain announced. No one questioned him.

Sam would never forget that final confrontation. Harry Traxton, the trusted bosun, and some of his most stalwart crewmen brought the accused Germans, Dieter Fleishman and Hans Wolton, before Captain Loring. Both men were in leg irons and chains.

Tall and rigid, with an entitled demeanor, sloping brow, and thinning red-brown hair, the hostile German appeared weasel-like. His shifty eyes bulged forward. He glared malevolently first at Zevia, then at Sam, as if to intimidate them.

Sam saw fine beads of perspiration on the man's upper lip. He alternately clenched and unclenched his fists as if preparing to strike. Harry and his men watched carefully.

Captain Loring stood up behind his desk. His authoritative figure gave credence to his unlimited power. His white uniform with the gold braid, the gold markings on his shoulderboards, and his intense focus on the prisoners seemed to goad Dieter to try to defend himself.

"You, sir," he raged at the captain, "would take the word of these two *Schwartzes,* this man and this woman, against the word of a German?"

His lips turned down in disdain as he gestured toward Sam and Zevia, who stood silent at the captain's right side.

The man's face reddened with seething anger. He continued to bluster, "You are crazy to listen to their lies. What proof do you have that what they say is true?" he sneered. "None! Only hearsay, and that is not permitted, not in any court of law."

Captain Loring turned to Hans Wolton, who stood, eyes downcast, as his cousin tried to plead their case.

"And you, sir," the captain said. "Is there anything you want to say?" The captain's manner was firm, but understanding. It was as if he knew Hans was the follower, not the leader.

"Nein; no, sir, I . . ."

"Don't say anything, Hans!" Dieter broke in. "It's our word against theirs! They can't prove a thing! We have done nothing! Nothing!" he insisted.

"It's not what you did, sir, but what you planned to do. Thanks to Miss Sinclair, we all know what you planned. As for proof—any man who'd pass himself off as a priest, a man of the cloth, well, such a man makes a mockery of God and mankind and cannot be believed. You, sir, could swear on a stack of Bibles as high as your head and I'd never believe you."

Captain Loring's voice deepened and his next words were measured and slow. "As captain of the *Eastern Queen,* for your seditious plans that would have meant peril to this voyage, I will set you both ashore on Desolation Island immediately!"

Dieter's face paled. Hans sucked in a hissing breath when he heard the dreaded words "Desolation Island."

Morning found the *Eastern Queen* moving blithely over the blue Pacific. Sam felt optimistic. He prayed that the worst was behind them. He loved mornings at sea. It was a fresh start, a new beginning, and he could revel in the promised excitement the new day brought.

The day's beauty astounded him, especially the peaceful blue of the water which changed colors as the wind and sunlight struck its rippling waves, first deep blue with flecks of white foam, then aqua-green as the movement of the ship caressed the waters. He noticed a silver flash as schools of fish leaped joyously in the freedom of the buoyant waters. Sam's thoughts turned to Zevia. Something bothered her.

Because Sam was making morning rounds, his back was to the main deck, so he did not see Zevia move behind him to stand at the ship's rail and stare out over the water.

He had been on watch since six in the morning. At ten, he was relieved, and he started below for a cup of coffee. As he turned to go below, he saw Zevia, motionless, at the ship's rail. The morning sun brought out the copper glints in her dark hair, and the great cape she wore clung to her lithe body. Suddenly, to Sam, she seemed so frail, so alone. Why did she stir his emotions? What was it about her that appealed to him, made him want to care for her, when it was obvious she had little interest in him? Her behavior was puzzling to him.

Sometimes she was friendly, other times she seemed cold and aloof. Her ambivalent behavior confused him. Would he ever understand her? And what was he to do about the rising interest he knew he had for her?

Thirteen

"Hope you're not too upset by our 'to-do' about the two men we left ashore."

When she heard Sam's voice, Zevia glanced up from the table where she and Jane were going over the little girl's lessons. Zevia was astonished by the quickening relief and pleasure she felt in Sam's presence.

He was dressed in fresh white trousers, and his white shirt, open at the throat, stood in marked contrast to his copper-brown skin.

"Good morning, ladies." Sam bowed in their direction. "How are you, Miss Jane?" he asked the child. Zevia thought, despite all that had occurred, Sam seemed self-assured and calm. She watched him as he helped himself to fresh coffee from the urn that Dorcas kept warm and filled on the sideboard.

"Am I disturbing you?" he asked.

"Oh, not at all," Zevia said.

Jane spoke up. "I'm doing my lessons because Miffy said if I finish and get my arithmetic and spelling right, I can go visit my daddy. Want to show him my lesson papers."

"I know he'd like that," Sam told her.

He smiled as Jane bent over her papers.

"You two seem to be getting along well."

"She's a pleasure to teach," Zevia responded.

"One thing, for sure, she's the apple of her father's eye," Sam said.

Zevia smiled. Sam thought her face lit up most attractively, and he felt reassured.

"I know that fathers are very close to their daughters," Sam said. "I'm surprised that your father let you leave him to come on such a long trip."

"My father loves me and knows me better than anyone else on earth," Zevia broke in impatiently. Her answer came swiftly, and the look she gave Sam made him realize he was treading on dangerous turf.

Alarmed, he stepped back. "Sorry," he responded quickly. "I just meant it's unusual to see a young woman travel so far alone."

Zevia looked directly at Sam as if to challenge him.

"I suppose you think I'm spoiled, or something like that. But that's not true. My papa was taken from his folks when he was only four years old as an indentured servant to a Prussian soldier. Papa told me that he always knew he had to apply himself and become a man. I'm proud of my father," she said in a no-nonsense tone of voice. She added, "Alexander Sinclair always said, 'You can't help what happens to you, but don't let circumstances beat you down.' "

What did she mean by "circumstances beat you down"? He decided not to ask, but to change the subject. "You told me before that Alexander Sinclair, the ship designer, is your father. He designed the *Eastern Queen!*"

"Yes, he did, Sam, and when he brought me to the

docks and realized that I'd be sailing on her, he said he felt better, knowing I'd be aboard one of his ships."

"Zevia, he's a gifted man. I love every inch of this ship. Her sails, her spars, the way she meets the sea, the way she seems to know what I want from her—even before I do myself, sometimes. When you have a free moment, I'd like to really show her to you, all of her. I know you'll love her like I do. My goal is to have a ship like this to captain myself someday."

Zevia could feel the tense excitement in Sam's voice. She thought he could have been talking about his love for a woman when he spoke of his dream. She had a dream, too—to be loved by a truly decent man who would love and accept her as she was, despite what she felt was an imperfection. She was flawed, she knew. Who would want her? She sighed and pushed the thought to the back of her mind. She'd hold on to the dream, no matter how impossible it seemed to her; it was all she had.

Sam had turned to replace his empty mug on the sideboard. He misinterpreted the worried look he saw reflected on Zevia's face.

"Don't know how those two blokes thought they could get away with what they had in mind," he said.

"Sam, they must have thought it was possible."

"Well, what they didn't know was that the captain has the only key to the hidden strongbox, and that's on his personal keychain," Sam told her. "They would have had to kill Captain Loring to get it, and that would be a mutinous act, the last thing you want on a ship. You were right, Zevia," he went on, "to tell us what you'd heard.

You saved us from what could have been the end of the *Eastern Queen* . . . the end of all of us."

Zevia shook her head modestly.

"It was the only thing I could do."

"Well, you did the right thing." He sighed, reluctant to leave. "I must get back to my duties. Remember to save some time so I can show you around the ship. You'll be a topnotch sailor yet," he laughed, "before this trip is over."

"I don't mind learning new skills," Zevia said. She thought for a moment before she went on. "Can you tell me how long before we reach Macao, is it, where the captain plans to leave us, Jane, Mrs. Fitch, and me?" she asked.

"With the excellent trade winds we have now, I expect between a week and ten days, perhaps. You'll be comfortable there."

"What's it like?"

"A beautiful cottage . . . lovely grounds, well-kept; a nice place. Mr. Shiuh, a *compradore,* a native agent for foreign business, had been a good friend of Captain Loring's for years. He owns the place. He's an educated, well-to-do Chinese man whose mother is from a rich Portuguese family. Captain Loring has been able to lease the cottage several times. Mrs. Loring and the captain honeymooned there, I was told, and whenever the missus would sail with the captain, she'd stay there when we went into Canton."

Zevia still had questions.

"How long before you come back to get us?"

" 'Bout two weeks, I'd say, if all goes well. Time to offload the goods on our ship and load up again with new products to take back home. No more than that. And . . . while we're in the harbor, our men will be shaping up the ship, new sails, new masts where needed, cleaning and painting, checking everything to see that all is 'shipshape,' so to speak, for our voyage home. But don't worry, Zevia, we'll be back before you know it. You won't have time to miss us!"

Sam gave her a big grin and was pleased when she reciprocated with a friendly smile of her own.

"See you later," he said, as he saluted and left the room. He was happy that he'd had his conversation with Zevia Sinclair. He hoped she would start to look on him as a friend. She was very attractive. Her peach-brown skin, dark, appealing eyes, and trim, rounded figure made him want to caress her. He could feel his admiration grow for her with each contact they had. He wished for more. He was proud of the way she handled herself with the crisis of the two miscreants. He wondered, what did she think of him?

The captain sent for Sam.

"Sam, my knee is worse than ever. It's painful even to touch, and I can't stand on it at all. Every time I try to put my weight on it, it gives way."

"Captain Loring, sir, I'm very sorry. What can I do to help you?"

"Much as it pains me, Sam, I'm stuck in this damn cabin. I'm obliged to leave the management of the ship to you. Most I can do is plot the course, relay the coordinates to you, and keep the ship's log."

"Maybe if you rest it, you'll get stronger," Sam hoped. "I know you want to be topside."

"Well, I do, but I'm depending on you. You'll have to see that the women are safely escorted to Mr. Shiuh's Three Flowers bungalow, and you'll have to represent me to Mr. Eng when we get to Canton. I could never climb those stairs to his office."

"But," Sam worried, "will they accept me, a man of color, do you think, Captain? Especially in your place?"

"Of course. You are an officer, and that means, in the eyes of the Chinese, that you are to be honored and respected. In addition, you will have my 'chop,' plus a letter written in Chinese that will further identify you as my representative. You know only officers may enter China. You'll do fine."

A week later Sam escorted the women to the bungalow on Macao. He told Mr. Shiuh about the captain's incapacitation, for which Mr. Shiuh expressed his regrets.

"I shall miss seeing my old friend," he said to Sam. "Please offer my sympathy for his plight. Do you think while he is in port he would care to be treated by my personal physician?" His olive colored face creased with worry.

"I will surely ask him, Mr. Shiuh. I know he'd be pleased to know that you offered. But I must tell you that there has been other trouble on this voyage."

"Ah so?" Mr. Shiuh's eyebrows raised in question.

"Yes; you must be on the alert. There are two men, Hans Wolton and Dieter Fleishman, who threatened to steal the ship's manifest. With that in their possession, you know they could have obtained a 'chop,' a permit to go up the river to Canton, and sell the ship's cargo. The captain ordered them put ashore at Desolation Island."

"The island off the coast of Chile?"

"The same. But as you well know, sir, many ships call at that port, ships from all over the world. So . . . wouldn't be surprised to see them turn up, even here in Macao."

"Why were they not arrested?" the Chinese trader asked.

"Because they had not actually *done* anything. You see, it was Miss Sinclair, the young Negro woman who's the governess for Captain Loring's daughter, who overheard them plotting. They were unaware that she heard anything. They were speaking German and did not know that she speaks the language as well. She reported what she heard to me, and when I informed the captain, he acted immediately."

"Removal of the culprits, eh?"

"Exactly. One of the them was a passenger, Dieter Fleishman, posing as a priest, so you see . . ."

"Quite clearly. I see we must keep the women close to quarters and be aware of comings and goings as well."

"That is what the captain wants, sir."

Sam dreaded the next few minutes. He would have to say goodbye to Zevia just when he was beginning, he thought, to break through her reserve. Just thinking about what was to come quickened his heartbeat. He wished there had been some opportunity for him to let her know just how important she was becoming to him. He had not even had a chance to show her around the *Eastern Queen,* as he had promised. His own responsibility had doubled with Captain Loring's bad knee. Sam was virtually the captain of the ship. He felt the weight of his burden, but what about Zevia? Was she at all interested in him? What would this separation do to their fragile relationship?

Fourteen

The *Eastern Queen* continued her mission and sailed up the Pearl River to Canton. She docked at the one-quarter-square-mile wharf, which was as far as any foreign ship was permitted.

Sam Cross, following the captain's directions, sought out the warehouse office of Mr. Kai Eng, the manager of the Hong, a trading guild.

When Sam saw the long staircase that led to the merchant-trader's office, he knew his captain could not have negotiated the rickety staircase.

"Sam," the captain said, "I know Mr. Eng to be a shrewd trader, but he is an honest one. He will charge an import tax, too. It will be outrageous from our viewpoint, with a large share of that going into his personal account, but we'll more than make up for it when we sell the Chinese goods back home. Now, Eng understands English and speaks it well. He was educated by English missionaries, so don't try to confuse him; you won't succeed."

The office was cluttered and dark. It took Sam a minute to adjust his eyes after the bright sunlight outside.

"Five blessings to you, Mr. Eng." Sam bowed to the stocky man who bowed in return, his face inscrutable upon seeing Sam instead of the captain.

"Long life, riches, a serene mind, a healthy body, and a love of virtue," Sam recited. "My captain, Webster Loring, of the *Eastern Queen* from New York, offers his apologies. He has sent me, first mate Samuel Cross, to transact business."

Mr. Eng, a short, squat man, fixed his piercing black eyes on Sam and smiled broadly. He had no visible concern that his visitor was of another race. He simply formed his fingers into a pyramid in front of his face and bowed.

"Good day, Mr. Cross. My sympathy is extended to your captain. I pray for good 'joss,' good luck, and a speedy recovery. Now, a sixth blessing to us all, Mr. Cross. More profit! Your captain has brought many goods?"

"I have the manifests, Mr. Eng. Fifty thousand silver dollars, plus . . ."

"Ah, yes." The man rubbed his hands in gleeful anticipation. Suddenly he paused, as if remembering something.

"Mr. Cross, I had expected your clipper ship to arrive here some weeks back. You were delayed?"

"I can explain, sir. We did have unexpected delays. A very bad storm which almost put us off our course, and I do believe, sir, it was at that time that the captain reinjured his knee. Our compass was damaged, and we had considerable damage to sails and masts, plus several crewmen hurt. And then we were further delayed by two mutinous men who had to be dropped off at Desolation Island."

"Ah, yes, bad 'joss,' eh? Well, I hope my news will not disturb you further. The mail ship from San Francisco came in before you. A packet of mail for you and your passengers is here. My clerk has it set aside."

Mr. Eng gestured to a young Chinese clerk, who bowed and handed the trader a packet of mail.

A letter on top of the bundle caught Sam's eye right away. He read the label. It was addressed to Miss Zevia Sinclair. Sam's heart almost stopped when he saw the envelope was edged in black. What would this message mean for Zevia . . . and for him?

He turned back to Mr. Eng, tried not to let his anxiety show.

"Shall we get to business, Mr. Eng?"

"It will be my pleasure, Mr. Cross."

Mr. Eng reached for his abacus. Both men were eager to conclude the trading—Sam so he could get back sooner to Zevia, and Mr. Eng so he could see his profits rise.

"The *Eastern Queen* contains several tons of iron and lead, steel, and copper, and also several hundred bundles of sealskins that were picked up off the South American coast. All told, sir, this cargo alone is worth five million dollars," Sam announced.

Sam watched as Mr. Eng's fingers flew over the abacus, expertly moving the beads as he totaled his own profit.

"Mr. Eng," Sam spoke quietly and respectfully, "I realize that you do not like to be hurried, but it would be a great and honorable favor to me and to Captain Loring if we could conclude our business within the next few days. I am eager, with the captain under the weather, so to speak, to be ready to return home as soon as possible." He did not add that he was worried about the envelope he had to give to Zevia.

"I will do my best, Mr. Cross. There are many coolies idle right now; my godown is empty. You can store all your cargo. An empty warehouse not make much money," he nodded and smiled. "Two, three days, empty *Eastern Queen* and place cargo in my empty warehouse."

"Good, Mr. Eng. Here is the captain's list of goods he wishes to reload on the *Queen.*"

Mr. Eng clapped his hands briskly three times and his Chinese clerk appeared.

In a swift Cantonese dialect, Mr. Eng recited Sam's list.

"Finest teas, yes, Bohea, Campoy, Souchong varieties, plus fifty bolts each of silks, *nankeens,* chinaware, porcelain, especially the blue-and-white pattern, and saltpeter, possibly brimstone as well."

The clerk wrote everything down, the delicate Chinese characters forming a list.

Mr. Eng stopped the clerk and held up his hand to get Sam's attention.

"Do you think your captain would like sandalwood carvings, beautiful works of art, very special, you know?" Mr. Eng added, always anxious to increase his trade.

"I believe he would, Mr. Eng. He told me to be open to any trading suggestions you might make. He said you are an honorable man."

"Shall be added to the list." Again Mr. Eng directed the clerk.

"Oh, yes," Sam said, "the captain especially wishes to buy several large bolts of camlet, the rich cloth made of camel hair and silk. It is much favored, he says, by the wealthy women in our country."

"Ours as well," Mr. Eng said dryly. "It is rare and

costly, but I will do my best to acquire some for you." Mr. Eng smiled politely. In his mind, the tax levy was adding up nicely. He would have a tidy profit from this transaction alone.

"One final request, Mr. Eng," Sam said. "The captain asks if you can secure a tiny Pekingese puppy for his young daughter. He realizes that it is a risky undertaking, the dogs being so favored by the Imperial House, but his wife has just died and his daughter is so young . . ."

"Please, sir, speak no more of this almost impossible request," Mr. Eng interrupted Sam's plea with a raised hand. "Impossible, impossible," he repeated, "but, who knows what a stupid coolie may smuggle aboard?" Sam noticed that the last request was not interpreted to the clerk.

Sam left the man's office, satisfied that he had done his best. He could hardly wait for the next several days to pass while the trade exchange was made. He was eager to leave this noisy, crowded gray-green land and sail out into the blue Pacific and home. Zevia was constantly on his mind.

He could see her, in his mind's eye, as she had walked down the ship's way to board the tender that took her, Mrs. Fitch, and Jane to the compound at the river's edge in Macao. Her face was almost hidden by the hat she had worn the day he'd first seen her on the wharf in New York. Before she stepped on the ramp, she turned to face him. Sam was disheartened by the wistful, forlorn look he saw sweep her lovely face. All at once, he sensed her reluctance to leave the ship. For a moment he had all he could do to hold back and not go after her. He didn't want Zevia to leave the *Eastern Queen*. He had not expected such feelings to come over him. He'd already admitted to himself that he felt an attraction to her, despite the fact that she had not encouraged him. Sometimes he felt she was almost ready to relax her guard, and then a barrier seemed to come become between them. What were her fears? he wondered.

Perhaps on the voyage home he'd have a chance to find out. Funny, from their first meeting, he had not expected to be intrigued by the beguiling young teacher from Maine, but somehow he was caught. She was independent, spoiled, willful, opinionated, but also generous, soft-spoken, unselfish, caring, intelligent, and beautiful. The whole mix made him want her. Sam sighed as he made his way back to the *Eastern Queen*. There was still the black-edged envelope in his possession.

Fifteen

Ships from various countries passed along the southern trade routes on their way to the Far East. Often, sailors, particularly those from unsavory vessels led by brutal captains, jumped such ships to find work ashore, many times as sealskinners. Sealskins and seal oil brought high profits to those engaged in the trade. Men were often "shanghaied," pressed into service from these many islands along the South American coast. The docks were busy, active, and frantically paced.

Hans and Dieter had been on the island for only a short time—long enough, however, to know they wanted to leave it. Angry at the disastrous turn their fortunes had taken, they sat together in a dark, greasy cantina, nursing drinks of rum and whiskey. The barroom was frequented by sealskinners, sailors, drifters—men who were coarse and rough, whose barbaric, cold-blooded work of clubbing seals to death and skinning them made them callous and cruel. Seeing their ruthless manners, their harsh language, and their bloody, greasy clothing, the fastidious Dieter shuddered as he watched them cajoling one another, releasing the workday tension. His eyes crinkled with disgust. He could see that these were men with no room in their lives for the softer side of life, the elegant life he longed to have.

As he gazed through the blue haze of tobacco smoke, listening to the babble of many languages, Dieter realized the men needed relief from their brutish, dirty labors, but he felt he didn't belong in such an awful atmosphere. Never had he expected to be dumped on a filthy, desolate island on the South American coast, inhabited by honking seals and coarse roustabouts. Desolation Island, off the Chilean coast, was not the destination he'd sought.

It was all the fault of his stupid uncle, who had denied him his inheritance. His mouth turned down in a sour grimace when he thought of the dead relative who should have helped him. He slammed his fist down hard on the greasy table, his anger almost too powerful to contain. The gesture startled his cousin, Hans, who stared at him open-mouthed.

"Was ist los? What's up?"

"Verdammt, Hans! How did the captain hear of our plans?" Dieter's eyes narrowed with hatred.

Alarmed, Hans answered quickly.

"I told no one, Dieter. I swear, no one! Who was there to tell? Only you and I talked that night."

"Someone had to have heard us," Dieter persisted. "You know what the captain said when we were hauled before him: 'I have been made aware of your plans to steal the ship's *frachtbrief,* bill of consignment.' How could he know that? And . . . we spoke in German."

Hans shook his head. "I tell you, Dieter, there was no one nearby. When we separated, after our talk, I did see the teacher, the *Schwartze* fraulein, near the wheel. She was speaking with the first mate, Sam Cross." Dieter's eyes widened as his mind absorbed his cousin's words.

"That's it! Hans, that's it! Don't you see? *She's* the one who overheard us!"

"But, Hans, we spoke only in German! The *Schwartze* . . ."

"I *told* you," Dieter explained patiently. "Her father was my uncle's indentured servant. He's the one who got what was rightfully mine! My uncle had promised my mother that he would help me. *I* could have been admitted to the school of my choice. Instead of high school and engineering school, I ended up with nothing! My uncle gave all to the *Schwartze* servant—said he 'owed' it to him. You know he speaks German like a native. I'm sure his daughter does, too. Think of it, Hans, accused by *Schwartzes* and condemned to this filthy hellhole by a bastard American captain!" He slammed his fist on the table again.

"So now, Dieter, you're the one with the brains . . . what now?"

Dieter's eyes squinted with his concentration, and he answered through clenched teeth.

"First, we're going to get off this damn filthy island. The smell of dead seals is going to drive me crazy! Got to leave this hellhole."

"To go where, Dieter?"

"Anywhere! We're signing on the next ship that comes round the Horn, no matter where it's headed."

Their luck improved. Within a few days a whaling ship, the *Fairhaven,* out of New Bedford, Massachusetts, signed them on as flensors. Always needing extra hands, the ship's captain eagerly accepted them as part of the flensing crew that sliced the thick slabs of blubber from the whale carcasses. Hans and Dieter had traded the grease and blood of seals for the blubber and oil of whales, but they were moving again, on the vast Pacific, toward another destination—Hong Kong—and . . . Macao.

Flensing was hot, greasy work. Huge, thick gray slabs of oily blubber had to be cut from the carcass of the whale. Flensors were straight, sharp knives that could slice through the blubber with ease. These heavy pieces were tossed into huge fire pots on the deck to boil or "try out" the blubber into oil. Young lads had the responsibility of keeping the fires hot. Like witches' cauldrons, the fires had to be maintained to a high degree to melt the fatty substance. One careless movement by a hapless youth could result in severe burns.

The captain of the *Fairhaven,* a man of enormous proportions, ran a very proper ship for a whaling vessel. When the greasy work was completed and the oil stored in barrels below deck, he always insisted on a thorough scrubbing and cleaning of the ship from stem to stern.

"Mayhap we make our living with grease and gore, but we don't have to live that way. Know some skippers do, but not *my* ship nor crew."

After the ship was cleaned, each crew member bathed and put on clean clothing. When the *Fairhaven* reached port, each man was allowed a half day of liberty while the oil was offloaded by laborers. The price of oil was quite high, and a handsome profit would be realized.

Both Hans and Dieter were eager to go ashore, to find some diversion. They had heard about the many brothels that abounded in the city. There were even boats of pleasure that floated in the crowded harbor, always available day or night to please any and all men, for a fee.

A brightly colored flower-festooned barge floated by and actually nudged the hull of the *Fairhaven*. The gang-plank, quickly lowered, was crowded with eager sailors trying to make their way to liberty and a better look at the young women who beckoned them from the inner recesses of the floating pleasure boats. There were in-toxicating fragrances of burning incense, and the tinkling sounds of bells wafted across the water as the *mama-sans* and their girls tried to entice prospective clients.

Most of the courtesans on the boats were no more than twelve or thirteen years of age. They moved like flutter-ing butterflies in their colorful kimonos and robes. They noticed the eager sailors. With their pearl-white faces and black kohl-rimmed eyes, they sent bewitching signals to the love-starved men.

Hans stared, disbelieving. His jaw worked spasmodi-cally and his mouth actually salivated. He could almost feel the delicate softness of a young, pliant body under his hands.

Hans's eyes widened in anticipation as he viewed the unbelievable scene. He turned to his cousin.

"Dieter, did you ever?" he gasped.

"No, never did . . . and never will," his cousin an-swered abruptly. "I have no time for dallying with women."

"But, Dieter . . ."

"No, Hans, no!" Dieter's face flushed with anger. "We must find a way to make some money here in Macao. You want to stay on a stinking whaling ship the rest of your life? We must find a way to improve our situation, get money somehow! Start thinking with your head, not your appendage. You're stupid if you are willing to spend your few pennies on women!"

Hans sighed. "It's been so long, Dieter," he complained.

"Steel yourself, man. When we make our fortune, you can have all the women you want."

Hans mumbled under his breath and turned his attention away from the tempting prospect. Of course, Dieter was right. He wasn't all that happy on the whaling ship, but . . . as soon as he had seen the women, he had been reminded of Helena Agnes. Was she still waiting for him in Hamburg? he wondered. Three years was a long time to wait for anyone.

The two men walked slowly along the waterfront, their path made more difficult by the teeming horde of humanity that they encountered. Portuguese, Chinese, Polynesian, and various islanders from the South China Seas—all sorts of languages and native tongues added to the confusion. Much attention was drawn to them as well. They stood out amidst the throng—two pale, light-haired "barbarians."

A small Chinese boy of about ten plucked at Dieter's sleeve.

"Come, sir, plenty good food, this way."

He tried to draw Dieter into a small sidewalk food store.

"Bug off, you beggar!" Dieter sneered, as he brushed the boy to one side.

The dockside noise and confusion bothered Hans, who hoped his cousin would find someplace to stop. He needed a cold drink, and he needed time to think about their "situation," as Dieter called it. Hans was still thinking about the women. Perhaps he and Dieter should go their separate ways. He'd always done well by himself. Indeed, he hadn't been happy with the turn of events since Dieter had shown up on the *Eastern Queen*. He thought he'd better start planning his own future. Dieter's so smart, let him make his own plans. Ah well, Dieter, always selfish, thinks of himself first, Hans thought. So Hans made his own decision. He would return to Hamburg—and, hopefully, Helena Agnes. Dieter never saw Hans move with the congested tide of humanity and enter the dark recesses of a small restaurant. When he finally did, Hans was nowhere in sight.

Sixteen

"You've done well, Sam," the captain said, when Sam gave his report. "The unloading and reloading of our new cargo should be completed in a few days. With good 'joss,' 'good luck,' as the Chinese say, we'll be ready to sail to Macao. There I intend to load more cargo, fresh fruit, vegetables, and the like."

"Great! Can't wait to pick up the women and head for home. Sir, have you seen all the ships in this harbor?"

"I know, Sam. It's a very crowded place. Don't think the Chinese realize how big, how far-reaching, the rest of the world really is. They seem determined to keep the world outside."

"From what I see, sir, the rest of the world is clamoring to get in. I see ships from England, France, Portugal, Holland—even one flying an Egyptian flag. Did you see that, ships from all over?"

"I certainly did. Patience, Sam. I'm eager to leave, too. I'm sending a message to Mr. Shiuh, giving him specific instructions about getting the women and my daughter to the dock in Macao."

"Glad you're satisfied with the business with Mr. Eng, Captain Loring," Sam said. "As you said, Mr. Eng is a very shrewd negotiator. I had quite an experience dealing with him. But he was interesting; I've never met anyone quite like him."

"A learning experience, eh, Sam?"

"It was."

Sam looked about the ship, obviously glad to be back aboard.

"Everything seems to be going well here, sir."

"Oh, Sam, yes indeed. The crew have been quite busy while we've waited in the harbor for the loading and reloading of the *Queen*. The hull has been cleaned, it has a new coat of paint, sailmakers have repaired some of the torn sails, and I've ordered enough new sailcloth that on our way back to New York the sailmakers can be busy making new sails. Without good sails, we're dead in the water, Sam. You know that."

"Quite well, sir. Without proper sails to take the wind, we can't move. I know how important they are, especially when one wants to make speed, like on a clipper ship."

Sam changed the subject to speak about what was really on his mind.

"Sir, about the women—think they've been comfortable with Mr. Shiuh?"

"Ah, Sam, I'm sure of it. Can't think of a more pleasant host than Mr. Shiuh. When my late wife and I spent time at Three Flowers bungalow, he was a most gracious host."

The captain's eyes glistened with moisture as he spoke. He was silent for a moment, as if reliving a poignant memory. He cleared his throat and continued to speak about his Chinese friend.

"I'm telling you, Sam, our slightest wish was his command. He has excellent taste in food and wine. There was always fresh fruit available, there were fresh flowers . . . beautiful orchids from his own hothouse, amaryllis, huge, colorful begonias, iris and azaleas; never saw such gorgeous plants. And Mr. Shiuh himself is a gifted raconteur, can speak eloquently on any subject. He's well educated, studied abroad, has a marvelous library. You know, his home is a virtual museum with fine art displayed throughout. No, Sam, I'm not worried. I'm sure the women are being well cared for—having an exciting time."

"I hope so. Be glad, though, when we can sail for home."

"That's a feeling we all share, Sam. No place like home."

Sam nodded in agreement.

"I saw Charles Morton and Dr. Fitch near some of the 'factories,' " Sam told the captain. "Charles located some other Harvard men clerking for American businesses. Told me that in a few weeks he planned to book passage on another ship for his return home."

"Ah, yes, he's an eager, ambitious young man. Wouldn't surprise me to see him move up the ladder quickly, once he gets his degree from Harvard."

"Dr. Fitch seemed to be unsure about what he planned to do."

"Well, can't say that I blame him, Sam. The church hierarchy either didn't know or didn't tell him that Mrs. Fitch would not be allowed to enter China, not even past the seaport. They're both disappointed, I'd say."

"Can't blame him, sir. But he might do his missionary work in Macao, or on one of the other islands," Sam suggested.

"Don't know," the captain mused. "I think he'll return home. He probably has to check with his superiors. But

Sam," the captain grinned, "how about a drink to an un-eventful trip home? We've earned it."

Captain Loring reached into a low cabinet beside his desk and brought out a bottle of brandy. He placed two glasses on a tray and poured some liquor into each one.

"Here's to continued good luck and a quick trip home, Sam."

The men clinked their glasses together before each took a sip.

Sam's thoughts turned to Zevia. He wondered why.

Sam left the captain's quarters and went to the top deck. He walked about the deck, noticing that Harry Traxton was supervising the crew in securing the thirty-foot-long boat on the hatch of the deck. This was the *Eastern Queen*'s largest boat, used to ferry men and cargo from ship to shore and back again.

"Hold there, ye stubborn laggard!" Harry yelled at one of the younger men. "Can't ye see whar yer moving? Steady, hold her steady, stupid lummox!"

The young tar's face was red from the exertion of manning the ropes that lowered the boat.

Sam grinned at the scene. Harry could whip even the tenderest "land-lubber" into shape; he had a way with the men. He was strict, but he taught them well, and the men knew it.

Sam drew deep breaths of the fresh sea air as he moved along the deck. He could smell fresh paint and saw that the sails were sparkling white, neatly furled until they would be needed. All brass fittings were polished to a brilliant satin finish; all ropes and halyards were coiled or tied in place. The deck was immaculate; it had been scrubbed until it was spotless. Sam loved the *Eastern Queen*. Would he have a ship like her one day? From what Captain Loring had said, he had a chance. He'd had the necessary sea experience, knew ships and the sea, and was willing to lead. All requirements for a captain, Captain Loring had said. As he stood watching the men at work, he thought again of Zevia. Why was the girl always coming into his mind?

A few nights later, all was ready.

"Mr. Shiuh, I'm not riding in that thing," Zevia protested, as she looked at the covered palanquin, the closed-in litter that the man had provided for their transportation. The men who were to carry the stretcher on their shoulders stood silent, expectantly awaiting directions from Mr. Shiuh, their employer.

"I've never ridden on the backs of human beings, and I don't intend to do so now! You must have a carriage or . . ."

"I agree with Miss Sinclair," Mrs. Fitch added, her face mottled with worried blotches. "Where is the carriage the captain promised to send for us?" she whined.

"Ladies, please, permit me to speak," Mr. Shiuh insisted.

"Please, Mr. Shiuh, please speak, but I'm not riding in that contraption. I'd rather walk to the dock . . ." Mrs. Fitch continued.

"Oh, no," the man interrupted, "that cannot, must not be permitted! Carriage not available, and I must carry out orders of Captain Loring. Is not wise for foreign females, begging your pardon, ladies, to be seen by public. Therefore must be hidden from all eyes in palanquin, for safety reasons. Much bad things can happen."

"Like what?" Zevia wanted to know.

"Not permitted to say, miss, but bad all the same. Please, ladies, I must obey the captain's orders. Must get you ladies and Miss Jane to ship before dark."

From his tone of voice, Zevia knew it was useless to protest further. Mr. Shiuh clapped his hands sharply and his men sprang to attention. The women were helped inside and the covers drawn. Zevia held Jane's hand. I'm going to be sick, I just know I am. What else can happen to me? Indeed, life must be very difficult for women in China, if they must be hidden like this, she thought.

Mr. Shiuh sighed with great relief when the bearers started forward. He had equipped two of his best, most loyal men with scimitars, and they had their orders to see that the foreign women reached their destination unharmed. They were to be taken to the mouth of the river to be met by the captain's crew.

"There will be extra rice for your families for the next year, and five yuan if your task is completed well," he had told them.

Extra rice to feed their three generational families was most desirable, and with five yuan, perhaps candles, even a new pot, could be bought. The men moved at a brisk pace, unaware of the discomfort of their passengers.

* * *

Sam, Harry Traxton, bosun's mate, and four young seamen manned the cutter to pick up the women at the water's edge. Sam was very anxious to see Zevia and finally head for home. Surely, after this voyage to China and back, the ship's owners, the Worrell brothers, would offer him a chance to captain his own vessel. Captain Loring was encouraging and thought it was possible.

"Sam, I know of no man better than you at handling a clipper ship and her crew," he had said. "Really don't know how I'd have made it, laid up like this, if I hadn't been able to rely on you. Can be sure I'll vouch for you—probably my last trip. If I lose my leg, won't be going back to sea, and if the Worrells need a replacement, you should be their choice."

"Thanks, Captain, but I'm hoping you can get your leg taken care of soon's we get back home. Must be some fine doctors in New York, sir . . ."

"Rather go home to Portland, Sam. You can take care of business with the Worrells in their New York office. I may stop in Boston for a medical opinion."

"Be glad to take care of everything, sir."

"Now," Webster Loring smiled at Sam. "Guess you can't wait to get Miss Sinclair back on board . . ." He smiled indulgently as a bright flush flooded Sam's face.

"It shows?" Sam asked.

"It shows, Sam."

"Guess some things like joy can't be hidden, Captain, not even from oneself. Never knew I could feel like this, but Miss Sinclair has captured my heart. Worse, I don't believe she realizes how much I care."

"Give her time, Sam. That's all she'll need. Time to

get to know you. She'll see what a fine young man you are."

"Certainly hope so . . ."

"Ummm," the captain mused. He reached for the black-bordered envelope from the packet of mail Sam had delivered.

"Tell you what, Sam. Perhaps *you* should be the one to give Miss Sinclair this letter. I see it's from her father; it no doubt concerns her grandmother. She's going to need some support, she'll need a friend, and I know you can help her handle her sorrow, so far from home and all."

"Certainly do my best, sir."

Sam sent a message by a passing seaman to tap on Miss Sinclair's cabin door and tell her that Mr. Cross was waiting for her on top deck to start a tour of the ship.

Sam waited for Zevia by the wheel. His own duties had been completed, but he was always most comfortable when he was up on deck. He looked out over the cobalt blue waters of Macao Harbor, and the white stone buildings with blue-tiled roofs reflected in the water. Would Zevia be able to take any comfort from the peaceful scene when he gave her the letter? Would she let him comfort her? An involuntary shiver ran down his spine. Despite the tranquil harbor, a foreboding feeling came over him. Someone's stepped on my grave, he thought.

Zevia had no idea how happy she would be when she returned to her small room on the *Eastern Queen*. In addition, she had not been prepared for the tumultuous leap her heart had taken when she'd heard Sam Cross's deep voice as he'd assisted her and the others to board the cutter.

"Good to see you, Miss Sinclair," he greeted her formally, "and you, too, Mrs. Fitch. Jane," he turned to the youngster as he lifted her aboard, "your father is waiting for you on board ship."

Zevia felt Sam's hand warm and firm under her elbow as he handed her over to Mr. Traxton.

"Careful, now; watch your footing," he said, as the cutter rocked slightly. "This will be only a short ride and we'll soon have you safely aboard."

"Dorcas, I've missed you so," Zevia exclaimed, when she saw the motherly brown-skinned woman who had befriended her. She flung her arms around the woman who responded warmly to her affectionate greeting. Dressed as a man, so the Chinese would not know a woman had entered the city, Dorcas had to remain on the ship to help cook for the men. Most always she remained hidden below deck.

"Good to have you back. How you been getting on?"

"Well, fine, but," she noticed Dorcas wore pants, "you've dressed like a man!"

"Only way I could stay on the ship to cook, dressed like a man, with pants and cap, and stay hid below, in the galley. But now, praise God, we'll be on our way back home!"

Lying in her berth the next morning, rocked softly by the rolling movements of the anchored ship in Macao Harbor, Zevia reflected on her feelings. She *had* been happy to see Sam. Was he aware of how much she had missed him? Could she keep the vow she'd made to herself not to trust another man, ever? Would she be able to extinguish the warm feelings that had rushed through her body when she'd seen his strong, handsome face after her exile at Three Flowers? What would it be like to have *his* hands touch her body, she wondered. You fool, she thought, didn't you have enough of that with Walton? But Sam is different, she argued to herself. He is warm and friendly, has no pretensions, and is considerate and sure of himself. She had noticed, too, the high esteem and respect his men showed for his leadership. And . . . he was the most attractive man she'd ever met. She couldn't describe the feelings she had when she was near him. Tall, with strong bones, sinewy muscles that moved smoothly as he walked around the ship, his head held high, he was not a man easily ignored. Zevia thought, he's like my papa—knows what he wants and won't rest until he gets it. She thought of his dark, far-seeing eyes that almost penetrated her mind as if he could read her thoughts.

Well, she had missed him very much when she was at Three Flowers bungalow. But now, back aboard the *Eastern Queen,* she would see him daily for perhaps the next three months. Last night, when he had helped her aboard, she'd seen a desire in his eyes that she had not seen before. *He had missed her!* The knowledge almost made her stumble on the gangplank. The overwhelming responding feeling of desire that she felt almost knocked her over. She wanted him!

Seventeen

Zevia hurried to the top deck. She was acutely aware of her mixed feelings as she responded to Sam's summons. She felt a joyous anticipation at being close to him again . . . but wondered, "What really do I want from this man?"

The sun shone warm and brilliant. A few crew members were busily coiling ropes on the deck. They greeted her pleasantly. The whole scene brought a sense of optimism to Zevia. Once again, she was safe aboard the *Eastern Queen.*

"Mornin', ma'am."

"Good morning," Zevia responded to the smiling men. She walked slowly to Sam, who stood engrossed in conversation with the helmsman. He had not heard her approach. Zevia noticed the way Sam's strong, muscular legs, outlined by his white trousers thrust into black boots, held his body erect as he balanced himself to accommodate the rolling, surging movements of the ship. His broad shoulders and slender waist intrigued her. His black hair curled around his neck and ears. Zevia knew she wanted to touch Sam, every inch of him. Her palms were wet. She brushed her hands on her sleeves to dry them.

Sam, Sam, she wondered, are you the man for me?

Sam must have sensed her presence. He turned quickly to greet her, and she broke off her welcoming smile when she saw deep concern on his face.

"I'm so sorry, Miss Sinclair."

He took her elbow gently and walked her away from earshot of the helmsman to the ship's rail.

"Captain Loring asked me to give you this letter. 'Fraid it's bad news. I'm sorry."

Zevia's fingers trembled as she took the black-edged envelope Sam handed to her. She recognized her father's handwriting. Suddenly, the sun-filled day became dark and cold as she read it.

> *My dear Miffy,*
>   *I found your beloved Oma very ill when I arrived back from New York. Oma kept insisting that she would never see you again. Despite the doctor's care, she died, asking for you. I need you; Opa needs you. Hurry home.*
>
> > *Your loving Papa,*
> > *Alexander Sinclair*

Zevia read the letter silently. Sam watched her closely, and when she looked up at him with tear-filled eyes, he instinctively held out his arms to her and she collapsed, weeping into them.

Sam held her close as she sobbed out her grief. He wanted to hold her forever, it felt so right.

Oma, she thought, I should have stayed home and never left. But how could I? You deserved a flawless granddaughter. I would have been such a disappointment.

She wept a few minutes more, then stepped out of Sam's embrace.

"I . . . I . . . I think I want to go back to my room," she told him.

"Sure you'll be all right?" Sam worried. "Should I send Dorcas . . . ?"

"No, Sam, thanks. I need to be by myself."

Tears continued to stream from her eyes as she walked blindly along the deck.

With her eyes clouded by tears, she stumbled along the ship's corridor as she tried to make her way to her room. She never saw the man who grabbed her, but she felt a large hand close over her mouth, stifling the scream that rose in her throat.

She was quickly blindfolded and pushed into a small boat. She could smell the fish odor and she felt the boat rock as a heavy body got in. She heard the oarlocks creak, then she heard the man's harsh, guttural voice.

"Quiet, *Schwartze,* or you're dead!"

Oh, God, she knew that voice! Dieter Fleishman! Where had he come from?

The man did not speak again. Zevia heard only heavy breathing as he rowed to a dock. From the sounds, she was at Boca Tigris, at the mouth of the Pearl River.

Jade Tulip, one of the *mama-san*'s most profitable girls, questioned the old woman. Her status gave her the brashness to speak.

"Why did the foreign devil bring such an ugly one to our pleasure boat? The whore's skin is dirty all over! She will bring only disgraceful notoriety to our place of business. And besides, he could have pleasured himself with one of us with skin like pearls," she pouted.

"Hush, do not fret, Jade Tulip," the *mama-san* said. "The foreign devil will pay well, and when he takes the girl away, we will fumigate the room and make it special again for our favorite clients, the French and the English officers."

Mama-san, Frosted Peony, did not dare tell the courtesan about the threat of the man's gun. She tried not to think of the cold steel he had thrust against her when she had allowed the crazy man with the black woman to enter her premises. She wanted to remember only the gold coins he had given her.

"Quick! Hide her! I'll be back! Don't let anyone see her!" And the foreign devil was gone, pushing the struggling Zevia into her arms.

Mama-san was strong and knowledgeable in the art of hand-to-hand combat. Nonetheless, she called for two of the younger women to help her subdue Zevia. If she played her cards right, she could become wealthy as a result of this transaction. There were always those men who would pay for something different. Girls of color, from India or Africa, were a rarity.

Jane Loring loved her new puppy.

"He's my best friend, Papa," she exclaimed.

"I'm going to call him Happy, because that's how he makes me feel."

She picked up the squirming puppy in her arms. "May I show him to Miffy?"

Mr. Eng had various contacts at the Imperial Palace,

and he had no trouble finding a willing coolie to smuggle the puppy to the captain.

The captain remembered that Sam was going to give Zevia her letter. He guessed she'd need time alone.

"You'd better wait awhile, daughter. She could be in her room."

But when Zevia did not appear for the noon meal, the captain asked Dorcas to check her room.

Dorcas looked into the small cabin. The berth was undisturbed. It was almost as if Zevia had never returned. The small suitcase she had brought back from Three Flowers bungalow was at the foot of the bed, but Zevia was not there. Dorcas gasped; she hurried back to report to the captain. Zevia had been missing since morning.

"She's not there, Captain!" Dorcas's worried face alarmed him.

"Well, where is she?"

"Don't know, sir."

"Sam," the captain turned to his first officer, "wasn't Miss Sinclair on the foredeck with you?"

Sam nodded, his heart pounded furiously in his chest. Where had she gone when she left him? Not so grief-stricken she'd fallen overboard?

"I . . . I gave her the letter. It was her grandmother—she died. Miss Sinclair wanted to go to her room . . ."

"We'd better search the ship."

Sam was halfway out of his chair before the captain had finished speaking.

God, don't let anything happen to her, Sam prayed

silently. His emotions churned turbulently as he realized the danger the woman he loved could be facing.

A few minutes later the dreadful news came. A thorough search from stem to stern, from top to bottom had been made. Zevia Sinclair was not on the *Eastern Queen.*

Later that morning, a scrawny, poorly clad Chinese boy ran up to the ship, thrust a note into the hand of a sailor on guard duty, and just as quickly vanished into the crowd. Captain Loring read it.

> *Have the girl. Before midnight tonight, leave $5000 in the basket hanging from the prow of pleasure boat number nine at Boca Tigris if you wish to see her again.*

Captain Loring saw the horrified look on Sam's face and gave immediate orders.

"Sam, take the pinnacle, our largest longboat, and as many men as you need to row to Boca Tigris as fast as you can. I'll send word to Mr. Eng and Mr. Shiuh to let them know about Miss Sinclair. Each of them is well-known in his community; I know they will help."

Sam swallowed hard, his jaw tense.

"Captain Loring . . . ?"

"Yes, Sam?"

"I hate to say it, but I believe I know who may have kidnapped Miss Sinclair."

"You do? Who?"

"It may have been Dieter Fleishman."

"You mean, one of the Germans we left on the South American seal island?"

"The same, Captain. I'll never forget the look of pure hatred he gave to Miss Sinclair when he left the ship. Somehow, he must have known she was the one who overheard his conversation with Hans."

"But how could he be here in China?" The captain frowned.

"He could have come in on that whaler, the *Fairhaven*. Whalers are always picking up extra workers," Sam said. "I think they stopped here for fresh produce, too."

"But my ship? How did he get on *my* ship?" the captain wanted to know.

"I believe I saw him. It was only a brief glimpse. Looked like one of the coolies transporting the fruits, vegetables, and teakwood on board here in Macao. He was bent over, like the rest. A coolie straw hat hid his face. There were so many of them streaming up and down, hurrying with their loads. I was talking with Harry Traxton and turned for a brief minute—could have been someone else, but I doubt it."

"Sam," Captain Loring broke into the tortured man's words, "if you're right, we can put the word out. I'll give a description to Mr. Eng and Mr. Shiuh. They'll put their workers on the alert."

"About the ransom," Sam spoke up. "I have money . . ."

"Sam, we'll work that out."

"Well, I, for one, will be on hand when the bastard comes to collect. If he's harmed Zevia, I swear I'll kill him!"

The captain saw Sam's clenched fists, saw the pain and anger in his eyes, and heard the anguish in his voice.

Sam loves the girl, he thought. She means everything to him.

"Sam, go! Go find her!"

"I will, if I have to search every vessel on this river! I won't leave China without her. I may not even be able to sail with you, but I swear, I'll find her and take her home if I have to build my own boat. Won't rest until she's safe. Captain, is my error in judgment going to cost Zevia her life?" Sam's face was a picture of agony.

"Don't think that, Sam. Take the men you need. Hurry!"

To himself, he thought, I have to face her father. An angry Black Hessian will be merciless.

She crouched into the dark corner of the cabin she'd been pushed into despite her valiant struggle not to submit to the will of her captors. Zevia was strong, and she fought hard. She scratched at the faces of the two young women who'd been told to lock her up. With every bit of strength she could summon, she bit, kicked, and pulled at their long black pigtails like a wild woman. Even so, one of them tripped Zevia's legs and she fell, despite her attempt to stay on her feet. They both ran for the door as Zevia scrambled after them. The door was slammed. Zevia cried aloud, "Oh, no!" as she heard a bolt being slid into place. She banged the door with both fists.

"Let me out! Let me out of here! Let me out!" she sobbed, and collapsed on the floor.

You're on your own, Zevia. There will be no one to

help you now. Papa not here, Oma is dead. You must find your way out of this fix or. . . .

Zevia did not want to think of the consequences she faced if she did not free herself from the confines of the boat used as a floating brothel.

Think, girl, think!

Zevia stared at the bowl of cold rice and the teapot of green tea that had been pushed into the darkened room. She had not heard any footsteps outside the door. It was only when a brief shaft of light came into the room that she realized the tray had been slid into the room. She rushed for the door too late.

Cold rice, cold tea. She wanted neither.

Her thoughts turned back to review the past weeks. Little did she know when she'd left the shores of Maine that so much could happen to her. She was far from home, in a foreign place on the other side of the world. Now here she was, alone in a dark cabin, in a strange country, with strange people. Even Mr. Shiuh's household staff had been kind and responsive.

"Missy, take more tea, please?"

"Missy need bath now?"

"Please, Missy, fresh fruit?"

They had tried in every possible way to make Jane, Mrs. Fitch, and Zevia comfortable.

But *these* people! Zevia knew there was only ill will in their hearts toward her.

She hadn't eaten since breakfast and wondered about the time. Surely it was getting close to evening by now. She could smell food being cooked, for an evening meal, she guessed. She wondered when the German would return. He was strange, too. Crazy.

Zevia got up and moved to the tray of food. She took a few sips of tea. It was cold, but strong. How could she get out of this situation? She remembered that the young Chinese housemaid in Mr. Shiuh's household had looked at her as if she were someone from a strange world. Well, Zevia vowed, she would show her captives "strange."

Eighteen

Harry Traxton came up on deck with a fresh mug of steaming coffee that he gave to Sam. He pointed to the forest of masts that peaked into the sky at Macao Harbor.

"This place is as busy as the harbor in Canton," Harry said.

Sam agreed. "Think it's because it's almost the last decent place for fresh fruit, vegetables, spices, teakwood, and the like that ships can load up with before heading home."

"Harry," Sam queried, "do you think the *Eastern Queen*'s got a chance to set a sailing record home to New York?"

Harry Traxton nodded.

"Don't see why not, Sam. She's a good ship, well-built, and we've got a good crew . . ."

Sam slapped his friend on the shoulder playfully. "Harry, *you've* seen to that. You've made the men into a first-rate crew. I say let's try to beat the record."

"What's the record, Sam?"

"Ninety-three days."

"I bet we can beat that," Harry wagered.

Sam pointed to a ship docked nearby.

"Isn't that the same whaler that was berthed near us in Canton?"

Harry leaned forward, "Yep, the *Fairhaven*."

"Thought it looked familiar."

Sam turned to face the deck. Many coolies and warehouse men were busily loading goods into the hold of the *Eastern Queen*. Like burdened ants, they moved back and forth from dock to ship. No one noticed a white man bent over almost double from the load on his back. His conical-shaped straw coolie hat hid his face, and his height was minimized by the bag of vegetables on his back. Sam watched for a while and then squinted his eyes tightly. There was something about the figure, the walk, the bent shoulders that bothered him, seemed heavier and more muscular than the average native Chinese. Ah, the Far East had many strange people from many strange places, he'd discovered. There were even Russians, Mongols, Tartars—any number of nationalities. Sam was too far away to see the telltale red hairs on the man's bare forearms.

Dieter Fleishman was deeply disappointed. He had walked the length of the dock, looking in vain for someone who might be able to help him. Several nations had official houses, but there was not one from his native Germany. In desperation, he stopped in front of a Dutch trader to seek help.

"Sorry, *mein Herr*," the businesslike clerk told him, "our charter with the Chinese tongs does not permit us to assist other nationals." He shook his head, "For my part, I would help you. People like you and me must guard against these infidels."

"I understand," Dieter said. "But perhaps you can help me all the same. I need a firearm of some kind."

The Dutch clerk raised his eyebrows and nodded.

"Now, my German friend, *that* I can provide. You know it is against the Chinese law for firearms, women, or whiskey to be brought into the country . . . but here in Macao," he shrugged, "if you have the money, I can provide you with a gun and ammunition."

Deeply disturbed by his poor circumstances, Dieter was returning to the *Fairhaven* when he became aware of a familiar sight. The tall masts of the ship he had been forced to leave, flags flying free in the gusts of wind that curled around them, caught his attention. It was the *Eastern Queen*. Tremendous activity surrounded her as hundreds of coolies moved almost as one machine, carrying packs and boxes of goods and foodstuffs up the gangplank and into the hold in the belly of the ship.

A plan formed quickly in Dieter's mind, so quickly he barely thought it out or reasoned. He acted. It was probably the brief, unexpected sight he had of Sam Cross and Harry Traxton talking together on the ship's foredeck. The two men, one his sworn enemy, appeared so self-assured and at ease with one another that Dieter almost choked on the sudden gorge of anger that rose in his throat. Vengeful anger took the place of clear thinking.

He clapped his hat on his head, grabbed a bag of vegetables from the nearest man, and clambered up the gangplank. After he left his burden in the hold, he returned, keeping a low profile as he pretended to be a working Chinese. He thought briefly of hiding in the hold, but his sense told him that such a foolhardy idea would not work. He'd be discovered. Still crouching low and scuttling along, trying to keep the same shuffling rhythm in his gait as the other men, he moved back in the direction of the gangplank. From the corner of his eye, he saw her.

Zevia, on her way back to her room below, her eyes filled with tears, never noticed the man whose footsteps paralleled hers until he grabbed her, a strong hand clapped over her mouth. Zevia fought, kicked, and tried to free herself from the iron clutches of the man's strong arms. He half dragged his unwilling victim as the startled coolies continued with their tasks. It was no affair of theirs if someone had a problem. Their task was to load the ship. Their credo was always, *Do as you are told, ask nothing, see nothing, say nothing.*

Once on the dock, Dieter tied a dirty rag around Zevia's eyes and with a bit of rope, tied her hands behind her back. He found a single boat nearby, and with his gun, motioned the lone Chinese fisherman to row.

"Boca Tigris," he growled at the petrified man. "Find pleasure boat number nine." He threw up nine fingers. The man understood at once: another foreigner, selling a woman for pleasure. He'd seen all kinds of women, all colors, sizes, ages. He rowed as quickly as he could. This red-haired *fan-qui* looked crazier than most.

Nineteen

The *mama-san* who allowed Dieter onto her boat believed him to be a client. She had not seen the girl he dragged behind him. He ordered brusquely, "Hide her. Keep her quiet."

He threw some coins at the woman, who realized at once what the crazy *fan-qui* wanted. Nothing these foreign devils did ever surprised her. Silently, she thanked the gods: if she managed this situation well, she could finally leave this life. Thank the gods as well that she had served many of the barbarians long enough to understand the man's English, even though it was accented.

"Hai, Hai!" She clapped her hands.

Several young prostitutes peered out from their quarters to see the *mama-san* struggling with Zevia.

"Take her below!" she screeched, as she aimed a swift kick at Zevia's head which stunned her. Zevia fell helpless on the floor and was dragged below by the giggling girls.

Frosted Peony, always directed by her practical Oriental wisdom, instructed her girls to conduct themselves as usual. She expected the foreign devil to return for the girl he'd paid her to hide. Perhaps she'd receive even more money when she presented her bill for food and lodging for the woman of color. However, it was important that business be conducted as usual, that regular preparations be made to receive their clients as they usually did each evening. Certainly, the regulars would be there.

Each woman bathed and perfumed her body with fragrant oils and had her lacquered hair twisted into an elaborate style. Each wore her most colorful robe.

Warm baths, moist towels, incense, plum wine, nectared fruits, soft candlelight, and the sound of tinkling bells awaited their clients. Every sensory stimulation imaginable had been anticipated and provided. Two decks on the houseboat contained small rooms for the sensual activity. As soon as the moon rose over the horizon and offices were closed, the men would arrive. Behind the colorfully ribboned latticework and flowered trellises, all was in readiness.

Suddenly, from the lowest deck of the houseboat, strange, wild sounds were heard. *Mama-san* did not understand a great deal of English, only what was needed for her business transactions. She knew what she heard was in the foreign devil's tongue, but to her ears, it sounded like a wounded, demented creature.

London Bridge is falling down, falling down,
  falling down.
London Bridge is falling down, my fair lady.
How shall we build it up again, up again, up again,
How shall we build it up again, my fair lady?

Build it up with wood and clay, wood and clay,
  wood and clay,
Build it up with wood and clay, my fair lady.

Zevia thought, they think I'm crazy. I'll show them! She was prepared to sing all eleven verses of the nursery rhyme and had reached the next line.

Build it up with iron and steel, iron and steel,
  iron and steel.

Each time she reached the last few phrases of the ditty, she sang a few decibels louder. She was practically shouting when the *mama-san* screeched to one of her girls, "Go, stop the heathen! She will send our clients away! Stop her, shut her up! Ay, ay, ye, ye, go! Do something!"

Two of the women who had locked Zevia down on the lower deck ran to the hidden area to slide back the locked bolt. No sooner had they done so when Zevia, still singing "London Bridge" at the top of her lungs, flung herself at the two astonished girls, who fled in fright from the wild apparition they saw.

Zevia's brown face was smeared with white rice. Her long black hair was coated with more rice. It looked as if worms were breeding from a decaying piece of meat.

"London Bridge is falling down." She screamed the phrase over and over as she thrust her hands out in front of her, flailing at the backs of the horror-stricken Chinese courtesans. Zevia did not stop, but ran blindly to the side of the boat and leaped. The oily black waters

closed over her head. She was free. The water was much warmer than in her native Maine, and she swam underwater until her bursting chest forced her to the surface for air.

She swam slowly, no longer in sight of the houseboat's occupants. The traffic on the water was unbelievable. Junks, sampans, houseboats with whole families, plus animals, living on them. Zevia looked about, tried to orient herself. Would she be able to find the *Eastern Queen* and safety?

Some of the flat-bottomed boats, steered by young men with long poles, carried farm produce as well as porcelain, teakwood, bales of cloth, and crates of tea. She swam by them slowly, not wishing to attract the wrong attention. She heard the singsong cadence of children's voices, heard fowl cackling and the honking of geese as an ungainly sampan floated by her. She searched in the dimly lit darkness and spied a dinghy tied to the end of the family's boat.

Silently and stealthily, she pulled herself into it. Luckily, there was a nondescript piece of soiled *nankeen* cloth in the bottom of the dinghy. She wiped her face with it.

Her thoughts turned inexplicably to Jane, the child she had learned to love. They had shared their motherless tribulations together. She thought of one sunny afternoon when the seas were calm. She and Jane were on the top deck, playing pretend tea party with one of Jane's favorite dolls, Hannah, as the guest of honor.

"Know what, Miffy?" Jane's voice was quiet and reflective.

"What is it, Jane?" Zevia heard the solemn tone in the child's voice. "Tell me what you're thinking."

"Well, when my mother died . . . for an awfully long time I thought it was all my fault—that she died, I mean. I thought I'd been bad . . . that her dying was all my fault . . ."

Zevia quickly drew the child close and hugged her.

"Oh, no, Jane. That's not true. You know, I thought the same thing. I thought if I hadn't been born, my mother wouldn't have died. But that's just not true. We're not to blame for anything!"

Zevia looked into Jane's face with a reassuring smile.

"Know what, honey? We've both got papas who love us more than *anything!* Why, your papa wanted you to be with him on this trip, and that's why we're *both* on the *Eastern Queen.*"

"And *your* papa said you could come, too!" Jane responded brightly.

"Yes, Jane," Zevia said quietly, "he did. He said I could come."

Lying there in the bottom of the dinghy, she wondered how her own father was doing. How she missed him, and how desperate she was for his approval.

And Sam Cross . . . she thought about him. Where did he fit into her life? She knew she was attracted to him. As much as she'd tried to resist his attentions, she could not deny to her innermost self that she was drawn to him. But if he knew of her imperfection, would he still want her?

The murky water was lit sporadically with flickering harbor lights, and Zevia tried to peer through the darkness to find something familiar. Where was the *Eastern Queen?* She sighed, took in deep breaths, tried to remove the seaweed and slimy water from her hair. She dried her face and arms as best she could with the ragged *nankeen* cloth. Her breathing became easier. She slept, too weary to think anymore.

Sam Cross finally found pleasure boat number nine. He had two revolvers and a small dagger hidden in the back seam of his boot. The other men were armed as well.

"Might not be my color, but we're all Americans," Harry Traxton told the others. "We'll not leave her here."

It was a dark night and nearly eleven-thirty before they reached the area.

"The bastard said 'before midnight,' " Sam told Harry.

"You going to put the ransom money in that there basket?" Harry pointed to a woven hemp basket swinging from the bow of the houseboat.

"Hell, no," Sam snorted. "Not money, but only some torn papers wrapped in a few bills to look like money. That bastard deserves whatever is coming to him, and I, for one, plan to see that he gets it!"

Sam's voice was low and determined. Harry Traxton thought he had never seen a man more relentless than the first mate was this particular night.

A row of small buildings faced the wide walkway that separated the buildings from the water's edge. Sam decided to station two of the men near the buildings. Some of Mr. Eng's men, as well as Mr. Shiuh's workers, mingled with the ever-present crowd of busy Chinese. Chinese workers hurried to local bars for a last drink before heading home; others waited in clumps, chatting with one another. It was a typical after-work crowd of workers doing what they did most evenings, try to barter, sell, and buy to make a small sum of money. Some were openly selling tea, cakes, porcelain, and copper utensils from their carts. Sam kept alert, looking over the crowd for someone who, despite attempts to look otherwise, would seem out of place.

Frosted Peony had finally summoned Niu Qua, her longtime lover and procurer. She needed his help.

"The girl escaped," she wailed to him, after she had served him his favorite tea and sweetcakes. "Soon the foreign devil with the red-haired arms will come back for her. I expect to charge him a thousand yuan for her board and room. He threw only a few coins at me when he left her here. Ye, ye," she moaned, "all is lost!"

Her lover grunted, sipped his tea, munched the cookies, and stared at the anxious woman.

"It was careless of you to let her escape." His voice was cold and accusing. "How did she do it?"

"She screamed some impossible gibberish just when it was time for our clients to arrive . . ."

"Stupid! You never thought to bind her mouth?"

"No, I . . ." The worried woman folded both hands in the voluminous sleeves of her robe, lowered her eyes, and shook her head silently. She was losing face rapidly in the eyes of Niu Qua, and she knew it. She had failed.

"What could I do?" she asked plaintively. "I sent two of the girls to silence her. When they opened the door, her appearance frightened them. She looked like an evil person. She had covered her face and hair all over with white rice. She screamed, pushed past them, and jumped into the river."

"Ummm. What did she take with her?"

The *mama-san* looked perplexed.

"Take? She took nothing. Wore only her strange undergarments, left her clothing behind."

"Good," Niu Qua said.

"Good? How do you mean, 'good'?" she questioned.

The man sighed. His voice was quiet and measured, as if he were explaining the situation to a child.

"Take one of the girls about her size and dress her in the heathen's clothing."

"But . . . she was dark-skinned!"

"Woman, must I think for you *always?*"

The procurer raised his voice.

"Rub some strong tea and a mud paste over the girl's face and hands. Put the crazy's clothes on her and give her to the foreign devil when he comes. But mind," he leveled a stern look at Frosted Peony, who was nodding her head, delighted by her lover's brilliance, "mind you do not turn her over until you have the money. Keep her in the shadows."

"It will be as you say," she told him. "There is one of the girls who wants to leave all the time. Cries that she wishes to marry a sailor. She will be the one he takes. You will be back later tonight? I expect my transaction will be concluded. All will be peaceful and serene for you here on pleasure boat number nine."

She backed away, bowing low, as the man rose from his cushion, stretched, yawned, brushed cake crumbs from his clothing, and left the salon.

"It had better be," he said brusquely. "Have the money ready."

He took no notice of the fawning female. Stupid old woman, he thought. Silently, he thanked the gods that he could shake the dust of number nine from his boots and relax at number twelve with his favorite, a delicate, ivory-tinted nubile maiden of incomparable beauty and sexual skills. Frosted Peony had been beautiful once, too, but now she was thirty. Much too old for his tastes, he sighed. Much too old.

Twenty

Dieter, wary and suspicious of the activity around him in the harbor, was compelled finally to hire a Chinese sailor with a one-man sampan to take him to the stern of number nine. He did not wish to be seen entering from the waterfront, as most of the clients did. The sailor was most agreeable.

"Ah, so, very nice pleasure boat," the sailor insisted. "Very nice. Best pleasure boat in Macao."

Dieter had no way of knowing that the sailor's intended worked on number nine. The couple was saving every yuan they could put by so they could be married as soon as the harvest had passed. The sailor often brought clients to number nine. Soon he and Pearl Iris, one of *mama-san*'s loveliest courtesans, would be together for life.

"Very nice place," the sailor repeated, as he steered his sampan toward the rendezvous site.

The crush of humanity on the street was almost too much for Sam to bear. Was this to be his fate, to be moved aimlessly throughout his life, propelled by the acts of others? Forced to live a life not of his choosing, but an accidental consequence of someone else's evil? He *had* to find Zevia; his life would be meaningless without her. He thought of the quiet, safe cobblestoned streets of his Nantucket Island home, how much he wanted to show it to Zevia. He thought of his exciting, vibrant life on the sea, the buoyant, invigorating life on the ship, the excitement of discovery, places, events, and mankind . . . so much, so very much. In fact, all of his life he wanted to share with her—the woman he loved. Where was she? The crowd surged along, hardly noticing the black officer and his bosun's mate, Harry Traxton. Life on the Boca Tigris waterfront was always chaotic and frantic, and strangers caused little concern.

Over the heads of the milling crowd, briefly lighted by a street light, Sam, with his height advantage, spotted a stumbling girl. She wore a dark brown woolen skirt and a pale pink blouse, the same clothing Zevia had worn when he'd given her the dreaded letter. But there was a heavy Chinese silk shawl almost completely covering her face. A tall white man was obviously forcing the resisting woman to move in a direction of his choosing. Dieter! And wait, was that Zevia?

"Harry! There he is! After him!"

Sam rushed, pushed blindly through the crowd. He could not let the pair out of his sight.

Unaware that he was being followed. Dieter pushed and prodded the girl. He had only one goal in mind: pleasure boat number twelve. That's where he planned to leave the *Schwartze*. Already she had cost him a thousand yuan, and the fool captain had not paid the ransom! The money trick was an insult, damn him! People must think Dieter Fleishman was a fool. Number twelve was only a few yards away. He'd sell her there—they would all pay for trying to best Dieter Fleishman.

"Dieter! Dieter Fleishman!"

"Wot iss?" Dieter turned quickly at the sound of his name being called, but he did not relinquish his hold on the struggling girl.

Sam's heavy hand fell on the German's shoulder. Dieter whirled as quickly as he could and reached for his gun as, still holding onto her arm, he pushed the quivering girl behind him. As he did so, the shawl slipped and he saw her face. He'd been tricked! She was Chinese!

"Where is she?" Sam demanded, as he ignored the gun in Dieter's hand. "What have you done with her? *Zevia!* Where is she?"

"Back off, *Schwartze,* or I'll shoot! I don't know where she is!" Dieter snarled.

With an anguished howl, Sam kicked the gun out of Dieter's hand. He reached for the man's throat. In the confusion, no one saw the Chinese girl melt into the night, into the arms of the sailor who had silently followed the German and his captive all night.

"You'd better tell me where she is, or tonight you meet your maker!" Sam hissed.

Sam's anger and hatred of the man reinforced his strength as he tightened his grasp on the man's throat.

Dieter's face dulled to a purple hue, his eyes bulging dangerously as he clawed at Sam's strong fingers.

Harry Traxton intervened.

"Sam, let's take him to the authorities. They can deal with him. Best we keep looking for Miss Sinclair."

Sam's fears rose to the forefront of his mind when he realized that Zevia's fate was still unknown. Oh God, where was she?

With Sam on one side and Harry on the other, the still choking Dieter was forced by the two men to walk to the American trade offices. He struggled to get away from their grasp, but Sam was angry and determined, and Harry Traxton carried the burly strength gained from his years of strenuous life at sea.

Dieter could not escape, despite his attempts to do so. They were not aware that they were still being followed. The infuriated Chinese sailor had pushed his love, the trembling Pearl Iris, into a nearby food stall, with whispered instructions to wait there until he returned. His stomach had churned with anger when he'd seen that it was Pearl Iris in the clutches of the red-haired foreign devil. It was one thing for his love to be paid for her graceful, artistic services as a courtesan, but it was quite another for his beloved to be pushed about against her will by the foreign devil like a common street cur.

Neither Sam nor Harry saw the shining blade leave the man's hand or heard the *thud* as it hurled through the darkness and found its mark between the victim's shoulder blades.

"Ugh," came from Dieter's lips. Sam and Harry felt the body sag.

"Come on, man, no hanging back now," Sam urged. He pushed Dieter forward brusquely. The body would have fallen to the street except that Harry still clutched one arm.

The lantern in front of the American trade building revealed the truth. Harry took a quick look.

"God, man!" Harry breathed, " 'Tis dead, he is!"

Then they both saw the knife in the man's back.

"My God, Harry! When did that happen?"

"Haven't the faintest . . . let's leave him here, get back to searching for Miss Sinclair."

"Can't do that, Harry. In less time than it would take to talk about it, these people would strip his body, sell his clothes, and throw his body behind a fishing shack to rot."

"He'd not be that caring for you, if the shoe was on t'other foot," Harry remarked.

"I know, he'd have no concern for me. As much as I despise him for what he's done, I can't leave him in the street."

"Ah, Sam, you're a good man. You know he wouldn't give a tinker's damn about you."

"Knock on the door, Harry. We'll let the authorities handle it. He probably has his seaman's papers on him, and they'll notify his ship, the *Fairhaven*."

The crowds of people hurrying about the dark waterfront paid no attention to one more commotion.

The two men waited in the darkness until the door opened. Two guards from the lighted doorway spotted the dead man and called for help from within.

Sam and Harry could do nothing more that night. They gathered their men and rowed back to the *Queen*.

Soon after the men talked with Captain Loring and gave him the report of their fruitless search, the word flashed through the waterfront and factories.

A "Black Pearl" has been stolen from the *Eastern Queen*. Zevia's description was given, with the added incentive, "Five thousand yuan for the one who returns her safe."

Mr. Shiuh's men and Mr. Eng's coolies spread the word. Every fishing shack, smoking den, and eating or sleeping establishment was searched. Fish stalls, vegetable markets, every factory, even wells and hidden caves—any conceivable space where a person could be hidden was checked and thoroughly searched.

Boats, sampans, rafts, skiffs, anything that floated

was searched. Five thousand yuan would support a three-generational family for many years. It was a singular opportunity. One that the foreign devil with the red-haired arms had made possible.

Twenty-one

Zevia was half awake when she heard a rooster's strident crow. Confused for a brief moment, she thought she was back home in Maine. Then she remembered. She sat up, bewildered, in the small dinghy and tried to get her bearings. From the stern of a houseboat, a large rooster with magnificently curled tail feathers of iridescent blues and greens looked at her with a beady eye. Then he clucked and continued his task heralding the morning's sunrise.

Zevia could see that her dinghy was attached to a very large houseboat with an active Chinese family aboard. She could also see chickens and piglets as well as children running about. From the singsong chatter she heard, there seemed to be a constant flow of dialogue between the elders and the children. Zevia's stomach growled when she smelled the pungent odor of food being cooked. She was about to be discovered.

"Nihao, hello, what have we here in our little boat?" Mr. Ling Po asked his eldest son.

"It's a woman, Father. She seems to be at home in our dinghy."

"Shi, shi, yes, yes, but not for long, son. I have been told of the Black Pearl missing from the foreign trader's

ship, the *Eastern Queen*. She could be the one! *Xia oxin,*
be careful, son, but get her into our houseboat quickly!
Jintian, today is our day of good fortune. How many
women of color does one see here?"

Mr. Long Po smiled a welcome at Zevia and beckoned
to her to board the houseboat by accepting his son's help.
Other faces peered at her from the houseboat.

God knows, I have to trust this man, she thought, as
she got into the houseboat. Surely a man with such a
huge family can't be all bad.

A younger woman came forward, a wide, friendly
smile on her face. She handed Zevia a blue quilted jacket
and a pair of baggy trousers. Zevia accepted the clothing
gratefully and dressed quickly, aware of her bleak appearance in her damp underwear.

An aged woman, obviously the matriarch of the family,
came forward, bowed, and offered Zevia a cup of tea.
Never had anything tasted so good. Following the
woman's gesture, Zevia bowed her thanks. She began to
relax. Maybe she would get back to the *Eastern Queen*.
The river was crowded with ships of all types, but where
was the one she wanted? Was the crew searching for
her? Was Sam looking for her? How did he really feel
about her, anyway? She remembered something else her
father had once told her: "It's who you believe you are
that counts, Zevia. You've got the bloody hardworking
independent folk in your family. No matter what others
may say, you know we are not inferior or less than anyone else."

She made a motion asking permission to move closer
to the brazier for warmth. The grandmother beckoned
her to sit nearby and offered Zevia a bowl of rice which

had bits of chicken and vegetables in it. Zevia ate every morsel of the food. She was starved.

Zevia thanked the woman, noticing the children, who seemed to range in age from toddlers to teens. The family chatted incessantly, and from their looks and finger-pointing, Zevia knew she was the topic of their curiosity. How could she make them understand what she wanted? She looked around for something that would help her. Finally, she spotted a flat piece of wood she had seen lying near the fire. She picked up a bit of charcoal and wrote *Eastern Queen* on it. She showed it to Mr. Ling Po and indicated that the words belonged on the side of the ship. She pointed to his Chinese characters on his houseboat, which meant *Eternal Happiness,* and tried to explain.

"I belong to the *Eastern Queen*," she said, and repeated *Eastern Queen,* pointing to her crude sign.

Suddenly, Mr. Ling Po's face brightened.

"E'ten Keen, E'ten Keen," he said, trying to pronounce the English words. He bowed and repeated the words over and over. *"Xie, xie, xie, xie.* Thank you, thank you," he said to Zevia. To his eldest son he gave quick instructions.

"Quick, up anchor! We take this woman to the *Eastern Queen.* She is the Black Pearl that was stolen! She will bring us much money! Hurry!"

Ling Po had seen the *Eastern Queen* in Macao Harbor only a few days before, when he had sold poultry to the ship's cook. He wasted no time in locating the clipper ship and maneuvered his houseboat alongside.

"Nihao, nihao, hello, hello," he called up to the young seaman he spotted on the deck.

The happy news swirled around the *Eastern Queen* like a whirlwind. Zevia had been found; she was safe. She was taken to the captain's quarters at once.

"Oh, Miss Sinclair!" The captain's voice almost broke with relief. "Am I happy to see you! Are you all right? We've been out of our minds with worry," he said, as he tried to stand to welcome the weary, disheveled girl. "Sam and Harry Traxton and some of the crew are still out searching for you."

"I'm sorry, Captain Loring, to have caused so much trouble."

"Nonsense, my girl! We are all so happy to have you back safe and in one piece. I know it's been a horrible ordeal for you."

"I guess, sir, I look a mess in these clothes, but I'm not hurt at all, only a little tired. The man and his family who brought me back were very kind. He seemed to know the *Eastern Queen.* Never thought I'd be so glad to see the ship . . . to be home again." Zevia almost choked with emotion.

"No happier than we are to have you back, my dear. I'm going to send for Dorcas to take care of you." He waved at his swollen knee. "Sorry I can't stand . . . this bum knee . . . but welcome aboard, Miss Sinclair! And I really mean that." He gave her a jaunty salute.

Sam's heart was heavy as he walked later that day along the dock to the gangplank of the *Eastern Queen.* He dreaded the report he'd have to give the captain that he, Sam, would have to abandon his post on the *Queen* to remain in China to search for Zevia. He would not leave without her.

He knew that could be considered a mutinous act, the end of his pursuit of his goal to captain his own ship, but he had no choice. His life was nothing without the woman he loved. He could not leave China without her.

He had barely put his foot on the first step of the gangplank when he heard a crewman shout.

"She's back, she's back, sir! Miss Sinclair's been found!" The young man's face was bright with excitement.

Disbelieving, Sam raced up the gangplank, his feet hardly touching the boards. The smiles, grins, and back-slapping from the crew made him realize the truth. Not only was Zevia back, the men all knew, even if he hadn't admitted it, how much she meant to him.

"Is she all right?" he questioned one of the men.

"Seems a little tired, sir, been out all night. A Chinese farmer brought her alongside little while ago. She's with Dorcas."

"Thank God!" Sam's usually firm voice cracked with relief. He rushed to Zevia's quarters.

Dorcas met him at the door to Zevia's cabin, her fingers to her mouth and a restraining hand to Sam's chest to slow down his impetuous momentum.

"Sh, sh, Sam. She's sleeping. She's safe now, just exhausted," Dorcas tried to reassure Sam.

"I've got to see her, see for myself . . ." Sam insisted.

Dorcas opened the door wider and Sam tiptoed in to see Zevia sleeping soundly. Never had Sam seen anyone more beautiful, he thought. Zevia lay quiet, her breathing

calm and regular. The soft light from the porthole radiated sparkling amber lights in Zevia's dark hair that lay
spread on her pillow. Her hands were tucked under her
chin as she slept on her side. Sam's heart beat so loudly,
he was sure he'd wake her.

Impulsively (he couldn't stop himself), he kissed her
forehead gently.

"I'll be back, Dorcas; take good care of her."

Dorcas snorted, "As if you have to tell me that! Boy,
get away from here!" She flicked her hand on Sam's
shoulder and was rewarded by a wide grin as he hurried
to the captain's quarters.

"She's sleeping now, Captain. From what I could see,
she's all right, thank God," Sam reported.

"Sam, she seems fine," the captain reassured him. "I
gather that she was in the water for some time. The family whose dinghy she was found in gave her food and
clothing. But Sam, I have to tell you, from the little she
has told me of her ordeal, Miss Sinclair is one strong,
resourceful young woman."

"One of the reasons I love her," Sam admitted in a
quiet, reflective voice.

"Finally have to own up to it, eh, Sam?" The captain's
tone was teasing but sympathetic.

"You bet, sir."

"Sam, I'm on your side. And now that Miss Sinclair
is safe aboard, we're ready to set sail. Give the orders to
'up' the anchor and we'll be homeward bound."

Each man had much to consider. The captain, while
not truly uneasy about relinquishing his authority to his
first mate, nonetheless felt guilty about not being able
to command. Much had happened on the way to China.
What lay ahead on the trip home? The captain had

known Sam for years. He had watched him mature from a young Nantucket Islander raised in a small, close-knit community into a man capable of dealing with untoward situations—like the Fleishman episode. And he was a man capable of tender love. His heart had been captured by a young woman with uncommon strength of character and resolve. The overriding factor was that the captain trusted Sam.

Sam, for his part, realized the great task that was before him. How would the men accept his authority? If they disagreed with a black man's leadership, the one who was really in command was still present, could still countermand any orders he might give. Sam thought, the captain wouldn't give me the responsibility if he didn't feel I was able to handle the job. He knows that I love this ship, I love this way of life, and he knows how much I love Zevia. More than almost everything else, I trust the man and his opinion of me.

"Sam," the captain voiced his thoughts, "I'll help you in any way I can. If you think you need me topside, I'll lash myself to a chair on deck."

"Oh, sir, won't be necessary. As long as you have faith in me, I'll do my level best not to let you down."

"I know you won't, Sam. I have every confidence in you, or you wouldn't be first mate. As soon as you're ready, we can shove off. We have our passengers already aboard."

"I didn't know we'd be taking passengers on . . ."

"Yes, well, Charles Morton is staying behind. As you know, Dr. and Mrs. Fitch are returning home to face the missionary board. The Worrells' nephew, their sister's son, Austin Worrell Talbot, been here for a year, managing the Worrell office—he is returning. And Sam," the captain winced as he tried to ease the constant pain in his knee, "believe it or not, Mr. Eng booked passage for two of his sons to sail with us. He wants them to see New York and Boston."

"That is a surprise, sir."

"I know. The Chinese have always said that they have all they need or want here in the 'Celestial Empire,' but I guess there is some curiosity after all."

"Finally realize that there's a big world out there," Sam replied.

"More than that, Sam," the captain said quietly. "Mr. Eng sent word to me that he was very impressed with you and your skills."

"Me, sir? I'm flattered."

"You're a good man, Sam. Mr. Eng saw that. Now, Sam, let's get her under way! Let's go home!"

Even from his seated position, with his afflicted leg stretched out in front of him, Captain Loring was able to give Sam a snappy salute.

Sam responded with his own salute and hurried to carry out the orders.

"Quartermaster, all hands on deck! Prepare to weigh anchor!"

He shouted to the officer at the helm, "Wait for sufficient speed, plenty of sea room, before you put down the helm."

"Aye, Harry," he called to the bosun's mate, "have your crew at the ready to ease the sails."

The sea chantey rose from the throats of strong, eager seamen as forty pairs of hands pulled on the great length of chain needed to raise the anchor.

Yo-o, heave ho!
Yo-o, heave ho!

The chanting cries helped them maintain their rhythm as slowly and steadily they hoisted the heavy cast-iron anchor that rose dripping from the murky harbor.

Not long after, a cry came. "Stowed away, sir," the crew leader reported. "Anchor's aweigh!"

Sam gave his order to the helmsman.

"Tack ship!" The graceful vessel changed her direction as the rudder was moved, and she turned slowly to come up head to wind.

Sam was everywhere, giving orders, watching the sails rise sparkling white to meet the wind.

"Pay out the yard on the mizzenmast," he shouted to the crew handling the sails. Sam watched with pleasure as the sail was hauled across the weather to push the stern around.

Sails flapped against the booms; ropes and halyards slapped vigorously against the rails; block and pulleys slammed against the masts; and the strident orders being shouted by the officers on the top deck to the crew and deckhands seemed to create a disorderly, chaotic scene. But in total command of a ship for the first time in his life, Sam saw only order and progress out of the frenetic activity.

Like an anxious filly at the starting gate, the *Eastern Queen* responded to her crew, shook free of her moorings, and sailed proudly out of the harbor. A lusty cheer rose from the throats of the men as the sails filled and caught the wind. She moved delightfully across the water.

In her room below, Zevia heard the rising cheer and

felt the responsive motion of the ship. Finally she was on her way to a future. *Of love?* she wondered.

Sam turned his face into the wind. This would be a truly different homecoming. This time he was bringing his own treasure home, a treasure of love, the greatest treasure of all.

Twenty-two

Sam made his way below deck to the captain's quarters to make his report and confer over the nautical charts with the captain.

"Take your bearings, Sam, and report the coordinates to me," he told Sam. "And another thing: if we can maintain satisfactory speed and avoid inclement weather, we may even set a sailing record from China to New York. Now, you know *that* would please the Worrells—might even earn us a bonus!"

"Sounds great, sir. Worth trying, I'd say."

Sam's mind was on Zevia. How had she managed to come through what must have been a horrible ordeal? Where had she found the strength, the courage, the stamina to outwit an evil man like Dieter? She was resting now under Dorcas's care. He could hardly wait to see her, to find out for himself if she was safe at last.

Sam was not aware of it, but he was in Zevia's thoughts. It seemed to her so long ago, after she'd learned of her grandmother's death, that Sam had held her in his arms. She ached for that feeling again: the intense flame that flowed through her body when Sam's strong, caring arms had held her. With her head resting upon his sturdy chest, his vibrant heartbeat echoing in her ear, Zevia felt loved and comforted. The feeling was one that had eluded her all her life. In the deep recesses of her mind she knew this was a different sensation. She wanted Sam. Did he want her?

When Dorcas had taken Zevia down to her room on the lower deck, she'd helped Zevia strip off the dark Chinese clothing.

"Let's get you a bath right quick," she muttered. "Hot water will be here directly. Child, you look a mess with all that salt water in your hair. I know one thing," she continued, as she poured the water brought to the room by one of the sailors, "one thing I know, you don't want Sam Cross to see you looking like this, though I know he's going to go crazy if he doesn't see you soon. Never saw that boy so worried. Thought he'd go out of his mind when we couldn't find you. Ready to tear this ship to pieces!"

"Honest, Dorcas?" Zevia questioned. "He was that worried about me?"

"Worried! Zevia, he was like a wild man! Told Captain Loring he'd jump ship, face mutiny charges, jail, *anything,* but he wasn't leaving this place without you! He was ready to kill that German, too, if he had to." Dorcas shook her head thoughtfully. "All the years I've known that boy he's been quiet, mannerly, levelheaded, interested only in ships 'n' sailing, but you sure changed him. Zevia, you know he's in love with you, that's all there is to it."

Zevia winced when she heard Dorcas's words. She looked up at her from the tub where she was bathing and frowned.

"Dorcas, I don't deserve his love," she said soberly.

Dorcas's reply came back quickly, impatience evident in her voice.

"Hush up, girl! Stop talking like that! Of course you deserve his love!"

"But, I . . ."

"Don't want to hear no 'buts.' I know what you're thinkin'. You made a mistake, but like I told you before, you ain't the first somebody to do that."

"But don't you see, Dorcas, I was always told I *had* to be perfect because my mother sacrificed her life so I could be born. I owed it to her, my Oma, and Papa always said . . ."

Dorcas snatched the facecloth from Zevia's hand, pushed Zevia's head between her knees, and began to soap the girl's hair.

"Now, that's the most awful thing I ever heard of, putting a burden like that on somebody! Know they're your kinfolk, but they are wrong. *Wrong!*"

The woman's words were emphasized by her vigorous scrubbing of Zevia's thick, dark hair.

"Your momma died because it was her *time* to die. Didn't you tell me they said she named you?"

"Yes, she said, 'Her name is Zevia.' Then she died," Zevia mumbled, beneath a cloud of wet hair.

"That's the way it was because that's the way it had to be. Perfect, hah! Nobody's perfect. I believe your problem is you try too hard to please others—your pa and your grandma. Don't you know there's only one somebody you can please? Yourself. Here, let me rinse your hair with this fresh water," she said.

Zevia leaned forward while the clean water removed the soap from her hair. Then she stepped out of the tub. Dorcas helped her dry off and wrapped a towel around her head. Zevia drew in deep breaths, relishing the sweet smell of the clean towels.

Dorcas continued to lecture as she pushed the small tub out into the passageway for one of the seamen to empty.

"Now, listen to me. Blow that 'perfect' nonsense out of your head. Believe me when I say Sam wants *you,* however you are. It's you he loves, not some 'perfect' somebody. And when he finds out 'bout all you've been through, he's going to admire you more than ever."

Zevia's eyes misted over.

"You really believe that, Dorcas?"

"Believe it? I know it!"

Dorcas had insisted that Zevia have a simple meal in her room and that she rest for the remainder of the afternoon. But Zevia wanted to leave. She wanted to breathe fresh air again, and . . . she wanted to see Sam. Through the porthole she could glimpse the setting sun. Would Sam be up on deck now? He had often told her that the prow of the ship was his favorite spot. He found peace and a spirit of promise whenever he stood there, sighting along the bowsprit of the ship as she sailed to distant horizons.

She felt an irresistible urge to see Sam. Perhaps then she would find some release from the restless turmoil in her heart. Did Sam really love her, as Dorcas had said? Could he forgive her flaw, her error in judgment, that had caused her such eventual misery? She had to know.

She hurriedly dressed and left the small room.

The golden Oriental sun was setting over the ocean waves, causing a fiery glow to emblazon the *Eastern Queen* as she rose and fell, meeting the waves with what to Zevia seemed to be joyous abandon. Zevia made her way topside, where she saw Sam standing. He was at the wheel, his back to her. Her heart beat frantically beneath her ribs.

She wondered how Sam was going to react when he saw her. Did he know anything about her past? Would he still have been willing to sacrifice so much for her if he ever learned the truth? Should she tell him? How could she, when she was experiencing difficulty trying to reconcile her own perceived imperfection? Her thoughts confused her. Would her life ever be right?

Sam's physical strength was evident to Zevia as she saw how his bronze arms grasped the wheel. The rugged vitality of his powerful shoulders and muscular back and the vigor of his legs, his total masculinity, almost took away Zevia's breath. Here, indeed, was a real man.

In the dusk of evening, he had not heard her approach.

"I believe another lesson is in order, sir," she said quietly.

He looked directly at her, disbelieving, his face bright with joy. With his right hand steadying the wheel, he reached for her with his left.

"Zevia! God, are you all right? I was so worried. Come closer, let me look at you!" The love in his eyes was unmistakable.

Zevia moved hesitantly to stand beside him. He pulled her close in an unbelievably strong hug. Zevia did not resist.

"Are you all right, truly?" His voice was thick with emotion as he searched her face for her answer. "You weren't hurt by that bastard Dieter?"

Zevia shook her head. "I'm fine, Sam."

"You're sure?"

"I'm sure."

"God, I should have strangled that brute when he first

came aboard the *Eastern Queen*. Had I known what an evil man he was . . ."

"Sam," she offered, "none of us can know what is in someone else's mind . . . what makes a person act the way he does."

"I still think I should have known . . ."

"Perhaps, but it's over now." She moved to free herself from Sam's embrace.

"Zevia, my watch is over in five minutes and I'll be relieved here. Wait for me on the forward deck, please. I have to know everything . . . *everything* that happened to you. You know I feel responsible."

Zevia shook her head.

"Well, I do," he continued. "I'll join you forward in a few minutes." His voice cracked. "You mean the world to me," he said softly.

Zevia shook her head again in quick denial, as if she did not want his spoken words to penetrate her brain. She was worried. How was she going to handle the next few minutes? Instinctively, she knew what Sam was going to say to her. And she knew, too, that deep inside her psyche, she ached for him to say the words that would set her free, the words that meant she was truly loved by a good, honest man.

She walked to the foredeck. The air was brisk, but felt clean and forgiving on her hot, flushed face. Her nerves were so taut that she thought she'd explode.

Feeling suddenly weak, she sat down on a coil of ropes. Was this the end of her life, or a new beginning? The next few moments would be crucial ones, she knew. She knew she had to face whatever came. Her father had told her once, "Miffy, nothing is worse than indecision.

Make the best decision you can, then live with it. No one can ever fault you for that."

So she sat on the coiled ropes and waited for Sam to join her. She gazed over the changing colors of the ocean as the sun sank beneath the horizon. A deep violet haze filtered over everything. Wild thoughts tumbled in her mind. Could she stop Sam from caring? Could she control her own feelings? The vow she had made so long ago never to weaken to another man was deserting her like a fading memory. This time, she wanted Sam's arms around her, wanted his mouth to cover hers, wanted his hands to caress her body. And more than that, she knew it was right for her to have those wants. She also knew she was helpless, caught, as in a net. She could not deny what was real.

Twenty-three

"Zevia." Sam's voice sounded quiet and reassuring to her as he came to where she sat waiting. He placed his hands on her shoulders. Their warmth penetrated through her cloak to her body like radiant heat, and Zevia jumped at his touch.

"Zevia, tell me what happened after I gave you the letter. You went back to your room . . ."

"Yes, Sam, when I left you." The memory of the moment distressed Zevia, and she hesitated for a moment.

"Take your time, my love," Sam said quietly. "I know it's hard."

"No, Sam, I'm all right. As I remember it, I was crying so hard at the time, I didn't see the man who grabbed me. The ship seemed to be so full of Chinese men, it was just swarming with them. Nobody helped me," she said plaintively.

Sam's face darkened at her words.

"I know, the ship was full of porters bringing our cargo aboard. No one tried to help you?"

"No one. It was as if they were blind."

"Oh, my God," Sam groaned. He reached for her hands. "Where did he take you?"

"To some houseboat, I think."

"Did you know it was what the Chinese call a 'pleasure boat,' for . . ." His face flushed, he hesitated to say the word.

"I knew it was some illicit activity, with all the girls, and the smells of incense and perfume. Anyway, he told an older Chinese woman to lock me up. I heard him say he'd be back for me."

"Zevia, you must have been scared to death!"

She shook her head.

"Sam, no, not scared—mainly mad. And I knew I had to get out of there! Somehow, even though they had locked me in."

"How did you manage to escape?" Sam wanted to know.

"I figured if I acted crazy, they wouldn't know what to do with me, and perhaps I could hinder their business somehow."

She could see Sam's eyes widen as she related her experience, the smearing of her face and hair with the cooked rice, the screaming singing at the top of her lungs, and her foot-stomping that rocked the boat.

"Zevia, that was clever. They didn't know what to do with you! Girl, you are something else. I'm proud of you."

"Sam, I had to take the chance." Zevia's voice was low and quiet. "I knew my life was over if the man came back for me. I believe he knew that I was the one who told you and Captain Loring about his plans to steal the consignment manifest."

"I blame myself, Zevia, because I think I saw Dieter when he came on board, dressed like a coolie. But I didn't expect to see a white man, so I guess I didn't.

If only I'd been on the lookout, as I've been trained to do."

"Don't blame yourself, Sam. And I want to thank you for all you've done to find me."

"Done! What I've *done?* For God's sake, Zevia, don't you know what you mean to me?"

He pulled her to a standing position to face him as he gazed intently into her eyes.

"Zevia, my dearest, don't you know that I love you? Since I saw you standing with your father on the dock in New York, there's been a pull between us that neither of us can deny. At least, I haven't been able to."

Zevia tried to stop the flow of his words with her hand over his mouth.

"Sam, you mustn't . . . you can't love me. You don't know anything about me . . ."

Sam turned her hand over to kiss her soft palm, sending frantic signals to Zevia's body.

"I know all I need to know, my dearest one. I know I love you, and want you to be my . . ."

Zevia tried to protest, her voice sounded weak to her own ears.

"Don't say any more, please, Sam." Her eyes sparkled with tears as she tried to move away from him. He held her closer.

"Look at me," he insisted. "You will see only love and respect for you in my eyes, Zevia. That's all you'll *ever* see. I see a woman of beauty, of strength and courage, the woman I love . . ."

"But, but . . ." she stammered. How could he love a flawed woman?

Sam stopped her protestations with a light tap on her opened lips.

"My love, my dearest." He hesitated briefly. "I know why you ran away from your family in Maine," he said quietly.

"You know? Did Dorcas . . ."

"No, my love," he replied softly, "your secret is safe with Dorcas. I know that you had been wronged, that you were an innocent victim who had been taken advantage of . . ."

"How?"

"I'll tell you. After that terrible storm, I was so worried about you I came below after things had quieted down to check on you. I saw Dorcas leave your room with the bloody sheets. My heart almost stopped because I was afraid that you'd been hurt during the storm. I was about to leave when I heard her at the door . . . yes, I admit I was eavesdropping . . . telling you that being a woman was sometimes a hard life and that you were not the first woman who'd been tricked. At that moment, I wanted to kill the bastard who'd caused you such suffering. My heart ached for you."

"Sam, I was so stupid, I didn't know what was truly wrong with me. Only knew I felt awful and didn't want to bring shame . . ." Tears flowed unchecked down Zevia's cheeks as unexpectedly she felt sudden relief from her secret burden.

"*Sh, sh,*" Sam crooned, as he kissed the tears from her eyes. "You told me once that you felt sorry that the captain's daughter had to grow up without a mother. You may feel you, too, missed a great deal, but to me, Zevia, you are my lovely, shining star, like those in the Southern Cross, and I intend to follow you for the rest of my days. You'll not shake me," he said defiantly. "And another thing," he added, "you will never, ever, be hurt again. By anyone," he promised. "And I mean that!"

He pulled her into his arms and raised her tearstained face toward his. He bent his head forward to kiss her. It was a sweet, tender kiss that moved Zevia. She sighed softly under his warm lips. Could she trust this man? She wanted with all her heart to believe him.

He had known her secret, but he had risked everything, was willing to give up everything, even his own career, his goal of becoming a captain of his own ship, a rare feat for a man of color, because he loved her. The answer to her unspoken questions came from Sam.

"Zevia, love will always overcome *everything*. You must believe that. I love you, and I always will." She could see that Sam's eyes were dark with desire. The sun had disappeared, and a full moon had risen into the black night sky. Everything Zevia looked at wore a silver sheen. It cast a soft purity over their intimate world.

Her legs felt too weak to hold her any longer. She did the only thing she could do. She put her arms around Sam's neck and pulled his face down to hers. It seemed right. His mouth was beside her ear as he whispered, "For me, our love is the only thing that matters. Zevia, my dearest, tell me you love me."

Zevia, wordlessly, turned her face to meet his lips. The glowing feeling that coursed through her body cast all doubt from her mind. This time, it was right.

Twenty-four

Zevia found Sam at the helm, busily instructing a young seaman how to handle the wheel. Zevia saw the earnest and painstaking manner Sam used in giving his patient instructions.

"The sea is quiet now, lad," he told the sailor. "That's why I'm giving you this lesson. There will be days when you'll hardly be able to hold her steady. Those days, when they come, will surely test you. Right now, all you need to do is keep her steady, keep an eye on the compass, north northeast and steady as she goes. Think you can handle her?"

"Aye, aye, sir," the young man replied with a brief salute.

Zevia stood in the darkened companionway leading to the deck aft. She was almost transfixed by the sight of Sam. She'd never expected such feelings to come over her. In the warm South Atlantic, the benevolent tropical sun smiled on Sam's bare torso. Zevia sensed a deep core of weakness in her own body as she gazed at him. She watched the finely sculpted bronze muscles of his arms and shoulders as he showed the young tar how to steady the wheel. Quivering nervously, she remembered the warm, secure feeling she had experienced the night before, when Sam had held her.

When she stepped forward into the brilliant sunshine, Sam noticed her. He hastily pulled on his white shirt, momentarily embarrassed to be partially out of uniform.

"Zevia, Miss Sinclair." There was no mistaking the joy in his voice.

Zevia's thoughts tumbled anxiously in her mind as she smiled at him.

"Am I intruding?"

"Not at all, not at all. Giving young Graham, here, instructions."

Her face flushed with inner tension. Zevia prayed silently, *Let him love me always!* This time she knew she had invested all she had in this one man—her soul, her mind, even the past she so wanted to forget. Could she be enough for a strong-willed, determined, single-minded man like Sam? Regret had no place, was not welcome in her life—not now. Not after she'd tasted the sweet elixir of love that they had finally shared.

"Can I leave you, Mr. Graham? I'll send one of the junior officers to supervise you while I take Miss Sinclair on a ship's tour. Just keep the course."

"Aye, sir."

As soon as they were out of sight of the young sailor, Sam planted a tender kiss on Zevia's cheek. She touched the spot with her fingers. "Today is a perfect day to show you the ins and outs of my *other* lady love," he said.

Zevia smiled. Sam thought she had never looked lovelier. She wore a blue and white gingham dress, decorated with a demure white collar. It brought out the lovely peach bloom of her complexion. Her trim figure was flattered by the long line of the dress.

"Not jealous, are you?" he teased.

"How could I be? She brought us together, didn't she?" Zevia threw back at him.

"She surely did, and I believe in all her wisdom, she knew we were meant for each other."

"Sam, I never knew the world could be so beautiful." Zevia gestured toward the blue-green ocean waves. She turned her face forward to the sun.

"Don't you know love makes *everything* beautiful?"

"Never thought so before, but I do now."

"My love, let me tell you something. My intention is that you see love and beauty forever."

"Is that a promise, Sam?"

"You bet. On my honor, by all that's holy, that's my promise to you."

With his hand under her arm to guide her, he led her forward, past the forest of riggings and ropes that rose upward to the sparkling white yards of the sails aloft.

"Come, my love. I want you to see your father's handiwork."

"My father loves his work."

"Anybody can see that your father knew what he was doing when he designed this ship."

"He used to say it was because Opa, my grandfather, once told him to look at a fish—sleek, slender—to see how it moved through the water."

"That's right. He knew a ship had to become part of the elements, water and wind. A ship can't be awkward or cumbersome; it has to 'clip' over the waves. Sometimes the weather changes and the ship has to adjust. Right now, today, we are lucky to have the warm Pampero winds off the coast of South America to push us north."

He pointed to the great masts.

"Once these were tall trees in the forest. Our mainmast is about a hundred thirty feet tall, our foremast a hundred twenty, and the mizzenmast is a hundred ten feet."

Zevia shaded her eyes with her hand as she followed his gestures. She didn't know when it had happened, but as they stood looking upward, she suddenly became aware of Sam's arm resting lightly around her waist. The sheer intimacy of it astounded her. She did not move, but only listened as Sam told her about the ship he loved.

Wherever they went, the efficiency as well as the beauty of the ship became evident. The joinery work was elegantly polished. Mahogany, rosewood, and beautiful maple had been used, especially in the public rooms of the passengers. The stark, spare cleanliness of the ship, brass rails and plates that gleamed with a polished brilliance, the decks scrubbed to a satin-finish patina, even the ropes, taut with strength, with no frayed or weakened strands—Zevia was impressed by the elegant *Queen*.

"You know, Zevia, it's strange how one man can make a ship respond to him, where sometimes another man can't. Depends on how she's treated. It's knowing the sails, whether they should be kept tight or loose, how they react to the wind, and how the ship wants to behave. I've seen some captains do everything in their power; the ship just won't act right. Another captain will have no trouble at all. His ship will outsail anything afloat. Eat out of his hand."

"It's almost like the ship is human," she said.

"Sometimes I believe they almost are."

He indicated the main hatchway ahead, which Zevia knew led to the main deck.

She was familiar with that part of the main deck below top deck because that was where most of the passengers' living quarters were, but below that was a companionway that led to the crew's quarters.

"Can't take you there, Zevia. This space beneath the foc's'le head is where the crew sleeps. Their galley and mess hall is aft of the mainmast. There's most always some crew sleeping during the day, those that were on first or second watch."

He directed her aft to another ladder. Now they were two decks below main deck. As they had moved about the ship, Sam was greeted by various seamen who snapped a quick salute and acknowledged Zevia's presence with a bow and "Ma'am."

"Sam, they really respect you, don't they?" she remarked, as he led her to the rear portion of the deck.

"I have tried my damnedest to earn their respect," he said. "They are not always willing to give it to a colored man. Somehow, you have to keep earning it, over and over. But most of the men know that there's not a task, not a single duty on this ship or any ship, that I haven't done."

"What do you mean?"

He grinned.

"Wasn't always first mate, second-in-command," he told her. "Only thirteen when I first shipped out. You'll never guess what my first job was."

"What did you have to do?"

"Take care of the chickens, geese, goats, cows, and pigs," he laughed. "They were kept in a roundhouse, quartered up close to the anchor head. That's so we could have fresh meat, milk, and eggs. A regular farmhand was what I was on board ship. Believe that's the lowest task on board. And I shipped out to see the world! Might as well have stayed in Nantucket if all I was going to see was the back end of a cow!"

"What a disappointment!"

"But I've done it all. From farmhand, I moved to the crew's galley, doing scullery work, then I worked with the cargo crew, then I moved to the quarterdeck crew, where I learned how to help with the sails and rigging. I've helped haul in the anchors, lashed them secure, trained and strained to do any and all tasks assigned to me—and to try to do them better than anyone else."

Zevia saw it then, in Sam's face, the innate strength that Sam Cross had been compelled to use to overcome the handicap of being a different color than his peers. Those experiences have made him the man he is, she thought.

"I've been there," he said. Continuing his reminiscences, "Going to sea is tough. Every man's life depends on each man doing his job and doing it right. Zevia, my love, no truer saying was ever made than 'All for one and one for all.' " He turned to her. "Well, what do you think of the *Eastern Queen,* now that you've seen her? All except the hold, because that's filled."

"Sam, I think she's beautiful!"

"So are you, my love," he said tenderly. "So are you." He tightened his arm around her waist as they stood at the ship's rail and gazed out over the blue-green ocean that the *Eastern Queen* rode so gracefully, so willingly. There was peace and fulfillment in the air.

Each was absorbed in his own thoughts. Zevia felt content at last as she stood beside Sam. His masculine strength radiated from his taut, firm muscles, his deep perception seemed to her to spring from behind his dark,

loving eyes that she thought could see beyond forever.
His love for her reassured her. All would be well.

Finally, she spoke.

"Sam, I'm beginning to think I know why you love
the ocean." She waved her hand toward the wide expanse
of water.

"Why, Zevia?"

"It's so large, so deep, so vast, it makes our human
problems seem puny. And the water can be so calming,
almost purifying—seems to bless us, don't you think?"

Sam considered her remarks as he looked over the
water. He reached for her hand and held it tightly.

"You're right, my love. The ocean can be forgiving,
but she can be very demanding at times. She can really
bring out the best in us. Guess that's one reason why I
love this life on the sea. I always have to do my best, be
counted as a man. I don't ever want to be less than that.
The oceans of the world expect that of me, demand that
of me, and that's what I want—to be seen as a man, the
same as any other."

Twenty-five

Jane had a severe cold. She had been coughing for several days, but one morning during the lesson, Zevia noticed that the cough had worsened. "Can't breathe, Miffy, can't breathe," she wheezed between coughs, and she seemed to turn her head away from the light.

Zevia put her arms around the sick girl in an attempt to ease her distress.

"Oh, honey, you're burning up! You're really sick!" It was then that she saw the spotted rash around Jane's ears and neck.

"Dorcas!" Zevia cried out.

The passenger galley was only a few steps away, and the moment Dorcas heard Zevia's frantic cry, she rushed into the dining salon. Her eyes took in Zevia's concern at once.

"What's wrong?"

"She's sick, Dorcas, awfully sick. Look at this rash."

"Ummm. Looks like measles to me." She picked Jane up in her strong arms and started toward Jane's cabin. Over her shoulder, she told Zevia, "Find Dr. Fitch. Tell him it looks like measles." Dorcas whispered to the moaning child, "Going to be fine, honey. Dorcas going to see to that."

Zevia's worry increased when she realized how seriously ill her charge really was.

She'd have to let Captain Loring know right away. She hurried down the corridor to find the doctor. Indeed, she thought, it might be better if *he* reported to the captain. He knew better about such things.

"Yes, Captain, Dorcas made the right diagnosis. It's measles, all right," the doctor said. "She has a high temperature, but since the rash has appeared, her temperature should get back to normal."

"I don't understand, Doctor Fitch. Except for a cold, Jane seemed fine at breakfast."

"Children pick up illnesses quickly, but most of the time they make a quick recovery. I think she will, too."

"I want her moved to be near my cabin, where I can see her, be near her . . ."

"I'll have Dorcas bundle her up and we'll bring her to you. Sir?" The doctor stopped before leaving the captain's quarters. "Sir," he asked, "you have had the measles yourself?"

"Long ago, Doctor, long ago."

"Good. I expect we may have more cases, especially among the young lads . . ."

"Away from home for the first time, eh?"

The next evening, both Sam and the doctor were summoned by the captain. The doctor spoke up to reassure the captain.

"Just checked your daughter in the small anteroom next door," he said. "I'm pleased to report good progress. Jane was able to eat some soup tonight."

"She does look better, poor little mite," her father agreed, "even with that awful rash."

"Well, yes, she's doing nicely, but as I expected, three of the young lads in the crew are sick. Have quarantined them in sick bay."

"Think there'll be more cases, Doctor?" Sam wanted to know. "Can't very well sail a ship without able-bodied hands, you know."

"I'm aware of that, Sam." The doctor nodded. "Just have to hope that the older ones are immune. It's the young ones who've come from isolated farms that are most vulnerable, the ones from down Maine or Nova Scotia, boys from sparsely populated areas. But we could have picked up the disease from our Chinese contacts," the doctor went on to say.

Down Maine! Sam's face flushed and a deep, worried frown creased his brow. Zevia was from Stoningham, Maine. Was she vulnerable?

He was eager to see her. Would she be at dinner that night? When Sam got there, Dr. Fitch and his wife were at the table. The captain had managed to hobble in on a pair of crude crutches one of the ship's carpenters had fashioned for him. He still wasn't able to negotiate the ship's ladders, but he could move along the passageway from his quarters to the dining salon. Austin Worrell Talbot, the newest guest, had been in China as a representative for his uncle's firm, and he was at the dinner table, as were Mr. Eng's two sons.

Mr. Talbot, a tall young man, nearly twenty-five years old, was a markedly handsome fellow with a ruddy complexion. His hair was prematurely gray and cut close to his head, much like a cap. He sat at the large table opposite the captain.

Sam noticed that first evening that the young man's dark brown eyes missed little. He seemed shocked by the presence of the Eng brothers at the table, one on either side of him, and it was apparent in his manner that he had not expected to share a meal with the governess or the first mate.

Sam could almost read Talbot's mind. His perplexity showed on his face.

What am I doing here on my uncle's ship with this strange assortment of people? There are only four white people at this table. How can this be?

Captain Loring, always an affable host despite his constant pain, sought the young man's attention.

"Gather you're glad to be going home. How long have you been away?"

"Almost two years, sir," Austin Talbot answered, as he helped himself to a large serving of roast turkey from the platter Dorcas was holding. "And, yes, I'm very eager to get back home. I understand the slave issue is being debated in Congress."

"That's a subject we avoid on this ship," the captain said. "Every person on this ship is free-born. I believe that's the way your uncles and their investors would have it," the captain said pointedly.

Despite the fact that Talbot's whole family were members of the Friends' Society, he had decided for himself that the restrictive standards of moderation and the simple life of the Quakers were not for him. He wanted money and all that money could buy. Trading was in his blood. He wasn't a Worrell for nothing. He would make the most of every opportunity.

He heard the distinct admonition in the captain's voice. Well, if that was the way he felt, so be it. He turned his attention to Mrs. Fitch. Later he'd deal with the blacks, the first mate and the young woman. She was attractive; he'd have to give her that.

Sam saw the assessing, proprietary look the man gave Zevia. He seethed inwardly. He'd have to watch Austin Worrell Talbot. Sam observed him closely as Mrs. Fitch responded to Talbot's query.

"Oh, yes," the woman told him, her plain face flushed by the young man's attention. "It has been quite a trip so far. We've had plenty of excitement. Miss Sinclair and I were quartered at Macao, and then, when we got back, Miss Sinclair was abducted. My, but it's been eventful, to say the least! Now, however, we are heading home, thank God."

"Glad you're safe, Miss Sinclair," Austin Talbot said to Zevia, who acknowledged his comment with a nod. "I understand that you're an entertainer, play the piano. Did you learn by ear?"

Zevia heard an implication in the man's voice that perhaps she played honky-tonk music that belonged in a saloon. Zevia answered quickly, "Are you familiar with Chopin's études, Mr. Talbot? There are twenty-seven of them. I'd be happy to play one for you after dinner, if you'd like."

Sam wanted to cheer out loud. Instead, he bent over his food. Good for you, Zevia, he thought.

Zevia did play the piano that night at the request of the captain.

"We've been through so much, my dear," he said. "If you wouldn't mind playing, I'm sure we would all welcome the diversion."

She played a Chopin étude, a Bach prelude, and a rousing march. The Eng brothers applauded enthusiastically.

They were impressed by the piano and the young woman. Austin Talbot stood up when Zevia finished her brief concert and bowed with mock deference.

"First rate, Miss Sinclair. Please accept my apology for my remarks about your ability," he said.

Zevia gave him a brief smile and asked the captain to excuse her.

"I'm a little tired, sir, if you'll excuse me?"

Sam followed Zevia when she left the salon.

"Are you all right, Zevia?" he questioned.

"Yes, I'm fine."

"I could have throttled that Talbot fellow, doubting your ability—didn't think you could really play. They never think we can do anything! You put him in his place right nicely, and I was proud of you."

Zevia said to him, "I can hear Papa's deep, strong voice even now. 'Practice, *Liebling,* practice. It's what will make you good at whatever you do.' And once a week I walked a mile to Madame Tobias's house for my lessons. She was as strict as my father. Guess now I'm glad I did study and practice," she told Sam.

As he escorted Zevia along the passageway, Sam's mind was on Austin Talbot. He would bear watching. There was something about the man that made Sam uneasy. Sam reached impulsively for Zevia's hand and drew it up under his arm. He pulled her close as they stood along the ship's rail in front of her cabin door.

"Zevia, we may have more rough days ahead of us. We're short of men because of the measles problem, and with the captain worrying over his daughter, we'll most likely be working much harder. I want you to be careful. I don't want anything to happen to you. And another thing—watch out for Austin Talbot. I saw the way he looked at you tonight, apologizing and all . . ."

"Sam, I'm not interested in Austin Talbot!"

"He's got his eyes on you, though. I can tell."

"Sam! I thought you cared about me, respected me, you said."

"I do, Zevia, I do, and I love you! That's why I want to protect you."

"Doesn't sound like it to me," Zevia protested. "First available man that comes into view, you think I'm interested in him. What do you think of me, Sam Cross?"

"Zevia," Sam pleaded, "you've got it wrong. I trust you. I don't want him to bother you, that's all. Now you're mad at me."

"Not mad, Sam. Disappointed and hurt, that's all. Goodnight."

She went into her cabin.

Sam stood for a moment outside the closed door. How could he make her understand how much he loved her, needed her—wanted her?

Twenty-six

Zevia did not appear for breakfast the next morning. Sam was very upset.

"Dorcas, have you seen Zevia this morning?"

"Yes, I stopped by her cabin earlier. She's sick, Sam. Doctor Fitch is with her now."

"Is it the measles?" Sam questioned worriedly.

"I think so, but could be more serious. She has a bad cough and a high fever."

"Oh, my God." Sam's face fell as he took his coffee with him to the captain's quarters. He found the doctor already there.

" 'Morning, Sam. I'm sorry, but I've already told Captain Loring that Miss Sinclair is quite ill. Evidently she never had measles, I'm afraid, and to make matters worse, she has pneumonia, a complication that could be very bad." He shrugged his shoulders. "Pneumonia often happens, and we know Zevia was in that filthy harbor for a while."

"My God," Sam interrupted, his brown face bleak with worry. "We are a thousand miles from the Leewards, almost two thousand miles from home port . . ."

"Wouldn't help us if we were within land," the doctor said. "They wouldn't let us into port, since we're under quarantine."

"You mean, because of the sickness we have on board?"

"That's correct," the doctor said. "We'd have to stay at anchor in the harbor."

Sam slammed his fists together in frustration.

"I feel so helpless. What can we do?"

"Move this ship with all possible speed to New York. And if either of you is on speaking terms with the man upstairs, I suggest you pursue that relationship. And while you're at it, ask for good weather."

"Good idea, Doctor," the captain agreed, "but I'm afraid we're in trouble on that score. I've been watching the glass. Pressure is falling, and we're headed straight into the Caribbean, a natural spawning ground for hurricanes." He shook his head at the dangerous prospect and then turned his attention to Sam.

"Sam?"

"Aye, sir." Sam focused his mind on the captain's words, but his thoughts battled in his brain with thoughts of Zevia and her struggle for her life.

He forced himself to listen to the captain.

"A great deal depends on you," the captain was saying. "How you work the sails, manage the wind and your crew. I know that Harry Traxton and our quartermaster, Ed Longdon, will support your decisions. I want you to keep heading north by northeast, but as soon as we've passed the Leewards, you should pick up the northeast trade winds. Head for the coast, expect the westerlies to come in, then make your heading northwest to home port."

"Aye, sir," Sam said.

The cabin was quiet as each man was considering his

role in the days ahead. The captain rested his chin on his hand as he sat at his desk, reflecting on their future.

"Gentlemen," the captain continued soberly. His face was stern, showing the seriousness of his thoughts. His shaggy eyebrows shielded cobalt-blue eyes that had looked at oceans all over the world. Now, they took in the measure of the two men standing in his presence.

"I'm sure each of you knows how exciting and thrilling the seas can be, but you know, too, how demanding they can be—can tear the very fiber of a man from his soul. The next few days may prove to be one of those times. God be with us all. Won't keep you any longer. Good day, gentlemen."

Sam's face was rigid with worry as he and the physician walked stride for stride out of the captain's quarters. Zevia was on his mind. She couldn't die; he couldn't lose her, not now, when they'd just found each other. He loved her with his whole being and truly believed she loved him. She was lovely, feisty, determined, and so desirable. He sighed audibly.

"Doctor Fitch, you know what Miss Sinclair means to me, don't you?"

The doctor nodded sympathetically. "I know," he said.

"I never thought, after her kidnapping, that anything else could happen. Thought I could protect her, keep her safe . . ." Sam's voice broke.

"I think that's how she got pneumonia, Sam. She struggled in that filthy water the night she escaped, for God knows how long."

He placed his hand on Sam's shoulder.

"I'm going to do all I can to pull her through, Sam."

"And I'm going to push every inch of sail on this ship

to the limit, God willing," Sam said through clenched teeth.

"Know you will. Got to check my patients. Let's pray that we'll see improvement in the next few days."

A full twenty-four hours had passed and Zevia was acutely ill. Dorcas had reported the dreaded news.

"Sorry to have to tell you, Sam, it looks bad. I'm so sorry, son," she told him. She rested her hand lightly on his shoulder. "She's worse."

Hearing Dorcas's words, Sam flung himself from Dorcas's side and rushed to Zevia's cabin. Once there, he could only stand in the doorway, transfixed by what he saw. He was unable to enter the room and could not tear his eyes away from the stricken girl.

He saw the bluish pallor around her lips, heard her harsh and labored breathing, and watched with pain of his own as Zevia moaned and twisted restlessly on the narrow berth.

Sam turned, his face taut with worry, to Dorcas, who had followed close behind him.

"Oh God, Dorcas, do something! Help her! Zevia means everything to me! She can't die, Dorcas! Not now!"

Dorcas heard the painful plea in Sam's voice and she knew from the unmistakable signs of grief on his troubled face that he was miserable. She couldn't tell him, but she was worried, too. Despite the efforts of Mrs. Fitch and herself, Zevia's temperature had risen alarmingly. The fate that Dorcas had feared for her patient had finally happened that morning: Zevia had slipped into a coma.

But when Dorcas looked at Sam's grief-stricken face, she knew she could not tell him. Not yet.

"Sam, you got any rum put by for the crew's grog?"

Sam was startled by Dorcas's question. As sick as she said Zevia was, why was she concerned about the crew's daily allotment of rum?

"Well, er, yes. We have several casks of rum in the locked cargo hold. Why do you ask?"

Dorcas nodded briskly.

"Good. Have the men bring a couple of demijohns of rum to Zevia's cabin. Tell them to keep the rum coming until I tell them to stop. I'll leave the empty bottles outside."

She placed her hand on Sam's shoulder in a gesture of support and tried to put hope in her tone of voice when she spoke.

"Got to get back to my patient, Sam."

"Dorcas, is there *anything* I can do?" Sam's anxiety almost choked him.

"Pray, son. Pray."

Dorcas turned away from Sam to enter Zevia's cabin. Poor lad. This crisis was hard for him to bear, she knew. She understood his helpless feeling.

"Sam," she prompted him, "get the rum. Hurry!"

When Dorcas closed the cabin door behind her, the scent of death seemed to assault her senses. The look of deep concern on Ellen Fitch's face said it all. The overwhelming heat from Zevia's body, the cracked fissures Dorcas saw around the sick girl's open mouth, and the labored breathing sounds alerted Dorcas to the impending danger her patient faced.

Ellen Fitch shook her head negatively.

"She's as hot as a fire chip, Dorcas. What can we do?"

If anyone had informed Ellen Fitch, proper matron, that she would ever become involved in the care and treatment of a "colored" person, and that her ally would be another woman of color, she'd have scoffed at such an unimaginable situation. Not her, a pampered physician's wife. But it was true. She was involved with the young teacher from Maine, and she cared about her deeply.

"Work, Ellen, that's what we're going to do. We're going to work and fight for this child's life!"

The time for formalities was over. Ellen and Dorcas were allies in a battle for Zevia's life and were now on a first-name basis as partners in the battle for Zevia.

Dorcas tore the sheets and blankets from Zevia's inert body.

"Let's get this nightgown off. We've got to leave her body bare. Here." Dorcas helped raise the garment over Zevia's head.

She ripped a towel into smaller pieces and reached for a small washbasin. She poured water into the basin and when she heard the thump of the demijohns outside the door, she brought them inside.

"Now," she poured some of the rum into the basin of water, "Ellen, we have to work and work fast," she told her.

She quickly soaked the torn cloths in the rum-water solution.

"Don't try to wring the cloths dry," she said to Ellen. "The point is, we got to cool her down as fast as we can. See, like this."

Dorcas demonstrated. With a moderately wet cloth in each hand, she drew the damp cloth down the sides of Zevia's hot face, turning the cloths over as they dried from the heat of the girl's body. She motioned to Ellen for two freshly wet cloths as she continued to apply the moisture all over Zevia's body. She moved the cloths in long strokes, careful not to apply any friction, along the girl's arms, legs, and abdomen.

"Help me turn her over so I can do her back, Ellen."

Zevia flinched and moaned almost inaudibly as the cool cloths touched her.

"It's all right, honey," Dorcas crooned, as she treated the unconscious girl. How much more can this young person take? she wondered. She continued to speak in soothing tones, as if Zevia could hear.

"We're goin' fight this ol' fever with all our might!" she promised.

That whole day the crewmen assigned to the task kept filled jugs of rum outside the cabin door. Dr. Fitch on his medical rounds stopped in to check the patient.

He shook his head worriedly.

"Keep up the alcohol sponges," he instructed the women. "And . . . pray."

For long hours that day, Ellen and Dorcas worked. Finally, Dorcas wearily stretched and rubbed her back. Her hands were chapped and cracked from the alcohol solution, but she dared not stop. She remembered too well Dr. Fitch's admonition.

"If we can't break the fever, we'll lose her."

Dorcas looked at Ellen and knew that she was nearly worn out. They had both been up all night.

"Go and get yourself something to eat, Ellen. Looks like you could use a breath of fresh air, too."

"Sure you can manage, Dorcas, for a while?" she asked. "I would like a cup of coffee, perhaps a roll. How about you?"

"I can manage. When you get back I'll rest a spell, maybe. Got to keep goin'."

After Ellen left, Dorcas focused her full attention on her patient.

"Look here, girl," Dorcas spoke aloud as if she knew Zevia could hear her. "Come too far now for you to give up . . . been through too much. You know Sam loves you. He's a strong man who deserves a strong woman. You *got* to get well! That's all there is to it. You hear me?"

She refilled the basin with more rum and water solution and resumed sponging Zevia's burning hot body. She checked Zevia's face for some sign of improvement. Nothing. She continued to lave the solution hopefully. There *had* to be a change soon. She had been working for hours.

She placed an empty jug outside the cabin door and picked up a full one. When she returned to Zevia, her eyes widened in amazement. She thought she saw something. Was it what she thought? She bent over Zevia and looked closer. Yes, by God, she had seen it: a faint bead of moisture on Zevia's upper lip. Dorcas then noticed a trickle of perspiration on Zevia's bare chest. The girl was fighting back. *Thank you, Jesus,* Dorcas wanted to shout. The fever had broken. The crisis was over. Zevia was going to live. Oh, thank God, she would have good news for Sam. The awful day had passed, and hope was again on the horizon.

Sam couldn't believe the good news. He kept repeating over and over, "Are you sure, Dorcas? Is it really true?

What did the doctor say?" The questions kept rushing out of his mouth as he searched Dorcas's face anxiously.

"When can I see her? I have to see her for myself."

"Later, Sam, later. I'll let you know."

Later that evening, after being bathed and dressed in a fresh dry nightgown, Zevia slowly began to regain consciousness. "Dorcas," she whispered, her eyes blinking with recognition.

"Right here, honey. Drink a little of this broth. Dr. Fitch is coming to check you, and I know Sam will be right behind him. Boy is about out of his mind."

Zevia could only murmur, "Sam," and then she fell asleep again. This time it was the normal sleep of one who has fought a battle and won.

The morning sun had risen with rose-gray streaks across the sky. Reflected in the ocean, it created an angry blush on the top deck as Sam went about his duties.

> *Red sky in the morning,*
> *Sailor take warning . . .*

Was this omen a warning of more dire consequences? Sam wondered. He had had little sleep, but being on deck at least kept his mind occupied.

He conferred with the seaman at the helm, checked the binnacle. Thank God, the compass was holding steady in the proper direction.

"Good morning," a voice came from behind him.

Austin Talbot was standing there. He'd obviously been watching Sam. He was about six feet tall, and this particular morning he wore a dark brown suit, a white shirt with a stiffly starched collar, and brown oxford shoes. He carried a brown derby in his hand and looked every inch the prosperous businessman. He stood staring at Sam. His feet were spread wide apart to balance and steady himself on the ship as it rolled over the ocean.

" 'Morning," Sam said agreeably. "Sorry, but you are not allowed to be up here on top deck. All passengers, for their own safety, must remain below on passenger deck unless specifically invited up here by an officer of the deck."

Austin Talbot's eyes were like twin orbs of grayish quartz as he glared at Sam. In an attempt to be intimidating, he spoke in a calm, icy voice. "Apparently you don't know who I am," he said.

"Oh, indeed, Mr. Talbot, I'm well aware that you are the nephew of the Worrell brothers, who own this ship," Sam replied quickly, not allowing his face to show his anger at the man.

"Well, then, I expect every courtesy due me. You are only a colored seaman, so I can go wherever I want."

"That's true, I *am* a colored seaman, but I'm more than that right now. I am the first mate, acting captain of this vessel on Captain Loring's orders." Sam's eyes never left Talbot's face. "And you are also right in stating that you can go anywhere you want, *except* here on the officer's deck of the *Eastern Queen*."

Sam saw the man's face redden with anger, saw Talbot's fists clench as he insisted on pressing his point.

"I can remain here if I wish. I have every right."

Sam's voice was measured and calm. His face betrayed none of the anger he felt toward the man who was trying to put him in his place.

"Mr. Talbot, your uncles pay a large insurance premium on a policy that agrees that if something untoward happens to the ship, its cargo, or its passengers, losses may be redeemed. The policy states there should be no one on the officer's deck without authorization, and I say . . ."

"And who the hell do you think you are to say anything?"

Sam could not mistake the arrogance of privilege in Talbot's voice and manner.

Sam controlled his anger. He took a deep breath and exhaled slowly. He was right and he knew it. He would not be intimidated.

"I'll tell you exactly who I am. Your uncles are waiting for this ship's return in their New York offices. You are on a ship two thousand miles away, in the Atlantic. They own this ship, mind you, but neither of them can help you get home. But *I* can. Whether or not you ever see them again depends on my skills as the acting captain, on my skills leading the men under my command, who have to man the sails and the riggings and work to sail this ship. So . . . with all due respect, sir, you'd better leave, or . . ."

"Or what, Mr. Cross?" Talbot's face became even more red and furious as he worked his jaw spasmodically.

"Or you will be escorted below. Quite simple, sir."

"This incident will be reported to my uncles," he snarled. "And mark my words; Mr. Cross, you will *never* set foot on another Worrell-owned ship, I'll see to that!"

"Be sure your report is correct, sir. I can assure you, 'this incident,' as you put it, will be recorded in the ship's log."

Talbot turned angrily on his heel and stomped toward the companionway to go below.

Sam watched him leave. He had no time to bother with petty annoyances like Austin Talbot. But he would make a report to the captain. A notice would have to be placed in the log. It was part of the record of the ship's progress, its speed, and any events of navigational interest, and the Worrells might be interested in their nephew's behavior.

Twenty-seven

Zevia, quite pale after her severe illness, was comfortably wrapped in her greatcoat. She stood beside Sam on the aft deck of the *Eastern Queen*. The weather had warmed considerably, and the *Queen* rode the Gulf current toward home. Sam had never seen Zevia more beautiful. Her illness had added a sheen to her skin that made her seem more desirable than ever.

It was a magnificent moonless night; millions and millions of stars studded the black velvet sky. Zevia instinctively drew in her breath and let it out slowly. Mirrored in the dark water, the heavenly brilliance was reflected on the ocean, making it a carpet of shimmering sparkles. The *Eastern Queen* rode the quiet waves regally and silently. Zevia felt weightless, almost ethereal, as she took in the beauty of the night. She felt Sam's arm around her waist. He, too, seemed mesmerized by the star-spangled spectacle.

He breathed into the sweet fragrance of Zevia's dark hair. "Zevia, my love, please say you'll marry me. I know you've been through a great deal, but I'm selfish enough to believe if you'll marry me, my love will be strong enough to protect you from everything. You know how much I love you, want you," he sighed into her hair, as her head rested on his chest.

"I know you love me, Sam." Zevia chuckled despite Sam's seriousness. "Dorcas said she thought you were going out of your mind when I was sick and that you'd drive her out of hers—after her every minute with so many questions, she didn't know up from down, she said."

"Well, she knew how scared and worried I was," Sam lamented.

"I know," Zevia said.

Sam turned Zevia's chin so that her face was turned up toward his. His eyes searched her face. Zevia shivered involuntarily as she recognized the love she saw in his face. She knew she loved this man and would always love him. No one else made her feel the way Sam did. She had no doubt that she, a girl from the rockbound shores of Maine, was loved by this man of the sea.

She said simply, "I will marry you, Sam. I love you."

Sam's lips moved lightly to Zevia's lips and she responded with her open mouth to receive his probing tongue. She was surprised by her own hunger. Her face flushed with the intensity of her feelings, and she gave herself up to the exquisite sensations that flooded over her body. Now, she thought, her promise of real love was coming true.

Two days later, on a clear Sunday morning, Captain Loring stood with his crutches and married Sam Cross, first mate of the *Eastern Queen,* clipper ship out of New York, to Miss Zevia Sinclair of Stoningham, Maine.

Ellen Fitch was delighted to be the matron of honor. Dr. Fitch proudly gave the bride away. Harry Traxton told everyone who would listen that "To be Sam's best man was the greatest honor o' me life." Little Jane, fully recovered, made a beautiful flower girl. The crewmen, those that were off duty, lined up in their best whites to form a path for the bridal procession.

"Stand up straight, man!" one tar admonished another who lounged against the railing. " 'Tis a weddin' you're part of, not a bloody cricket match."

"Give over yourself," his mate replied, "know it's only the extra pint o' grog that's on the mind o' the likes o' you!"

"Half a day's rest ain't bad, either," another sailor said.

"Well, look alive, now. Stand straight! The piper's started ' 'Ere comes the bride' . . ."

Forty sailors stood to attention as Zevia walked between them on the arm of Dr. Fitch toward Sam, who waited with the captain beneath the bowsprit. She was a vision of loveliness, Sam thought, as he waited for her to reach his side. He didn't realize until later, when he took her hand in his, that he'd been holding his breath.

Dorcas had shortened and altered the ice-blue silk damask dress that Ellen Fitch had given Zevia. She groomed Zevia's thick dark hair into a beautiful coronet braid intertwined with thin blue ribbons to form a tiara-like coiffure.

Then Dorcas stepped back to view her handiwork.

"Child, you look like the Queen of Sheba!" She clapped her hands with delight. Ellen Fitch agreed.

"That dress was made for you, Zevia. It's my gift to you, and when we get to New York, you must go straight to a photographic studio to have your picture taken. They can do such things there now, I'm told."

Later that night, the captain wrote in his log the following:

Course steady, fair winds. Making nine knots. Today married first mate Samuel Cross to Miss Zevia Sinclair. May fair winds, smooth sailing, and a safe harbor be theirs always.

> Signed,
> Capt. Webster Loring
> Eastern Queen, *out of New York.*

Sam was delighted to show Zevia the berth in his first mate's cabin that had been built especially for his predecessor, a man of substantial girth.

"I know it's only a seaman's berth, my love," he explained, "but when I have command of my own ship, when I am captain, you'll have fine quarters, a large, comfortable fourposter bed, a chest of drawers, a dresser and mirror . . . you will go to sea with me, won't you, Zevia?" Sam pleaded. "I could never bear to leave you ashore."

He gathered Zevia into his arms and tilted her face toward his. His lips pressed gently on Zevia's welcoming lips. Zevia closed her eyes as she savored the strength, the masculinity of her husband.

Sam suddenly stepped back. Zevia opened her eyes quickly.

"What's wrong, Sam?"

The question in her eyes made Sam even more uncomfortable. He hesitated for a moment, unsure how she would react to his explanation of his abrupt behavior.

"You've been through so much, my darling Zevia. I don't want to hurt you. Perhaps we'd better not . . ."

Zevia knew immediately what was in Sam's mind.

"Better not! Sam," she said, "I'm not made of cotton candy! Don't you *want* me?"

"Want you?" Sam almost choked on his response as he pulled his bride close. "Want you! Oh God, Zevia, I don't know when I *didn't* want you . . . ever since I saw you step aboard the *Eastern Queen* with your father. You were the most beautiful woman this Nantucket Islander had ever seen! Want you? Even now, I can hardly believe you're my wife."

"I'm yours, Sam. Captain Loring said the words that made us one. Remember?"

This time Zevia reached for Sam's head, pulled his face forward, and kissed him. Sam opened his mouth and with his tongue caressed and stroked Zevia's tongue and mouth. Zevia moaned in ecstasy.

They were interrupted by a tap at the cabin door.

"What? Who's there?" Sam questioned, his voice thick with emotion.

"Open up, boy!"

Dorcas and Josiah stood grinning outside. Dorcas carried a tray covered with a white cloth, and Josiah carried a broom.

"Know the captain married you two up real good," Josiah said, a wide grin all over his warm, dark face, "but me and Dorcas want you to 'jump the broom,' just like the oldtime folks did."

Zevia giggled and Sam slapped Josiah on the back.

"Come on in, friends," Sam said. "Come in."

Zevia smiled at Sam. "Are you willing, Sam?"

"Willing and able." He grabbed Zevia's hand and they both stepped over the length of the broom held by their old friends.

"Now you're really married," Josiah pronounced. "We

ain't going to stay long, know you want to be by your-selves, but me and Dorcas had to let you know how we feel. You're like our own children."

"Sure are," Dorcas agreed. "Brought you a little sup-per. Fried chicken, biscuits, potato salad, and greens. Even made you a little fruit cake."

"Snuck a bottle of the captain's wine, too," Josiah added.

"Josiah, you and Dorcas got to share a glass with us before you go," Sam insisted.

"Just a dram, boy, that's all, then you two are on your own! Got more important things to do than drink with two old people," Josiah smirked.

Dorcas took a quick sip from her wineglass, then hugged Zevia. "Be happy, child," she said simply. She kissed Zevia gently on her cheek.

Zevia's face flushed with emotion, and tears sparkled in her eyes. "Thank you, Dorcas."

Their friends said a quick goodbye and were gone.

Alone again, Zevia asked Sam, "Are you hungry?" She waved her hand toward the tray of food. Sam shook his head.

"Only for you, my precious—only for you."

He reached for her hand and led her to their bed. Zevia's fingers trembled in Sam's strong, capable hand. With gentle care, Sam removed the ribbons from her dark hair, releasing her crown of hair until it sprang and un-coiled in thick waves around her shoulders. Then he took her face in his hands and kissed her gently. The touch of her husband's lips on hers washed away Zevia's doubts.

Sam Cross knew all about her, but he loved her without reservation.

Zevia closed her eyes as Sam lowered her gently to the bed. There was to be no turning back now. At last the future was here.

"Oh Sam, Sam, love me," Zevia moaned.

She gasped as his fingers touched her skin, moved gently to cup her breasts, while his mouth sealed kisses over her mouth, eyes, cheeks, and neck. Zevia clasped her arms around Sam's neck to bring him close to her.

"Beautiful, beautiful Zevia," Sam crooned, as he nibbled her ear.

Suddenly, Sam stopped, strode over to the table, and extinguished the kerosene lamp that hung over it. Zevia watched as Sam pulled at his clothing. In the dim moonlight from the porthole, she saw her beloved husband move to her side. His tall, strong, firm body, muscles contoured and well-shaped, were visible in the soft light.

Zevia quickly pulled her nightgown over her head and tossed it on the floor. Then she extended her open arms to her husband, who growled a soft murmur as he reached her side.

"Oh God, Zevia, I love you so much!"

Later they lay, bodies entwined, as a benevolent midnight moon filtered through the porthole and blessed their union.

Twenty-eight

"Captain Loring sends his deep regrets, sir," Sam Cross told Angus Worrell, when they met in the merchant's New York office.

Angus Worrell raised his eyebrows with unspoken questions when he saw the young officer who reported to him from the *Eastern Queen*.

"Is he sick? Why didn't he report? Why send you, first mate?" Disappointment was evident in his voice.

"The captain has been plagued by an old injury to his knee. It was reinjured during a storm. He's been off his feet, almost unable to stand for some time now. He's on his way to Boston, to a hospital on Beacon Street. I only hope they can save his leg. He fears they may have to amputate," Sam told him.

"I certainly hope not. Fine man, Captain Loring."

"Yes, sir. I owe him a great deal," Sam agreed. "I've brought the ship's log, as well as all the papers and manifests concerning the cargo. He directed me to give them to you."

"Yes, yes, let's have a look at them," the eager merchant said, impatient to check his profits.

He quickly scanned the manifest in his hand. "Say, tell me, young man," he said, eyeing Sam, "word has come to me that the *Queen* may have set a record. Is that right?"

"I believe she has, sir. We got word as we rounded the point at Sandy Hook that we could have done so. Here is the captain's log."

Angus Worrell turned quickly to the last entry.

"By George, here it is! Eighty-nine days and twenty-one hours from Canton to New York!" His broad face beamed with pleasure.

"Yes, sir," Sam said proudly, "the side trip to Macao and our troubles there were taken into account in the actual calculations."

"Sorry business, that kidnapping of Miss Sinclair . . ."

"Mrs. Cross, now, Mr. Worrell, sir," Sam said proudly. "We were married on board ship by the captain. She's waiting for me now in a hotel just off South Street," Sam told him.

"Sinclair, hmmm. Sinclair, you say? Is her father by any chance Alexander Sinclair, ship designer?"

Sam nodded. "He is, sir."

"Well . . . well, congratulations! You've married into a fine family. He is one of the best ship designers I know. It's due to his design of the clipper ship that we've been able to command such speed. I'll be damned, son-in-law, you say. Did you bring the *Eastern Queen* home under your command, son?"

Sam hesitated to say anything. He didn't want to put the captain in a poor light, but he *had* been acting as captain.

"Well, you could say I was acting captain, sir. I had Captain Loring to turn to for advice, you know," he said quietly.

"I hear the modesty in your voice, Mr. Cross, and I

admire that. You know, as Quakers, we don't give a fig about a man's color, only his worth. Hear you hail from out of Nantucket, and from what you tell me, Captain Loring himself may not be able to go to sea for a while. However, we have a new ship coming down the ways in Portland. She's a Sinclair-designed clipper." He grinned at Sam. "Think you and your bride would be interested in seeing her launched?"

"We'd be delighted! Be a grand chance to meet my father-in-law. I really admire his ship designs, but more than that, sir, I want him to know how much I love his daughter. My wife says her father calls her his 'Liebling Miffy.' "

"It will be several weeks before the ship'll be launched," Angus Worrell told Sam. "Take the time to go to Maine. You should at least have some sort of honeymoon. In the meantime, we'll get the *Eastern Queen* ready to sail. Would you agree to sail with her again?"

Sam smiled. "I'd like that very much, sir, as long as I can take my wife with me."

"Of course, of course, by all means," the portly merchant agreed. "A ship's captain can always take his wife along, if he wishes." He watched for Sam's reaction.

"Do you mean that, sir? That I'm to be captain?" Sam almost choked in his excitement.

"You come highly recommended, young man. And that means a lot. One moment . . ."

Mr. Worrell strode to a side door leading into an inner office.

"Come in, A.W.," he said.

Sam's eyes widened as he saw Austin Talbot step through the door, his hand outstretched as he reached for Sam's hand.

"Welcome, Captain Cross," he said, as Sam accepted his firm handshake with one of his own.

"A.W. has told us how you stood up to him on the *Queen*. You're the kind of man we want," the merchant explained. "A man of conviction."

"Yes, indeed," young Talbot said. "Told my uncles that they'd never find a finer man to captain a ship than Sam Cross out of Nantucket. Congratulations!"

"Thank you, Mr. Talbot." Sam turned to Mr. Worrell and extended his hand. "I shall do my best to serve you, sir," he said. "I shall try not to disappoint you, on my honor as a seafaring man from Nantucket."

"I know, Sam, the home of the Quakers. I am sure you'll do your best. Your father-in-law is the best ship designer I know. Sailing with us, you'll have the finest ship under your feet, and we'll give you the finest crew possible."

"Sign up the ones already aboard, sir. Never saw a grander bunch of men. I'd be honored to work with them."

In a hotel room near the waterfront, Sam eagerly gave Zevia the good news.

"I've been made captain, Zevia! Captain!"

"Oh, Sam, how wonderful. It's what you wanted."

"Well, I owe it all to you, my love."

"Me? Why do you say that?"

"Mr. Worrell was delighted when he realized that the *Queen* had set a record. Eighty-nine days and twenty-one hours is a long time. You know," he smiled tenderly at her as she watched him undress for bed, "Captain Loring thought I wanted to set a sailing record. Well, I did, after all the things that happened to us, but more than that, I had a better reason."

"You did? What?" Zevia asked.

"Captain Loring had a big, beautiful bed in his quarters. Big enough for two. You know, my love, how cramped we were even in the first mate's large berth. Not that I'm complaining, but—I had a good reason to set a record!"

"Really, Sam, what?"

"Indeed, I had promises of untold pleasures waiting for me, and they are all here in this hotel room." He looked directly at her.

Zevia had already undressed for bed. She wore a white cotton nightgown. Her hair was braided into a crown on top of her head. Sam had told her he liked it that way because it made her look regal and queenly. She walked over to the bed and lowered the bedcovers. She knew what Sam meant. At last they were together in a quiet, comfortable, warm, loving space of their own.

Sam watched Zevia as she moved. He took in every lovely motion, every exquisite line of her body as she walked around the bed, folding down the coverlet. He felt as if he would melt from the fervent heat that flamed his body. His pajamas and bathrobe were stifling him. He did not want to frighten his wife, but his unfilled ardor was mounting within him. He knew he could wait no longer.

He opened his arms to his wife.

"Come, my love," he invited.

Wordlessly, Zevia went to her husband. With a swift, sure motion, Sam picked her up in his arms and carried her to the bed. He laid her down gently, turned out the light, then he took off his robe, never taking his eyes from her face. He slid into the bed beside her and took her in his arms.

His voice was husky with emotion.

"Zevia, do you know how much I love you? When I thought you were lost, perhaps out of my life forever, I wanted to die. Without you, I'd have nothing to live for."

"Oh, Sam, please don't talk! Love me. We've waited, *I've* waited, so long . . ."

Tears squeezed from beneath her eyelids when she realized that she was asking for love. The knowledge frightened her that she could have spent her whole life not having known the love to which she was entitled— had lived for.

Sam's mouth found hers and covered it. Zevia gasped from the sweetness of the kiss, the promise of a forever she'd always wanted. She murmured little sighs as she responded to her husband.

He reached for her and pulled the nightgown over her head, shrugged out of his pajamas, and tossed everything on the floor. The heat from their bodies rose as their lovemaking compelled them to seek, to touch, to kiss, to revel in their oneness.

Sam buried his face between Zevia's breasts as her quick inhalations let him know that she was responding to a sensation that had been denied her. Sam reached to caress her rounded breast and he kissed its rose-hued nipple with great tenderness. He did not want to hurry or frighten Zevia. The few intimate moments they had managed on the ship now seemed only a prelude to the joy that waited for them. He knew his heart would be satisfied at last.

This night he wanted to share with Zevia the soaring love that he felt for her. He stroked her body with his hand, first her soft abdomen, her silky thighs and the delicate mystery beneath the dark triangle of soft down. Zevia moaned and moved her body in ecstasy as she responded to her husband's loving touch. Her thoughts roamed wildly through her mind as her body answered his touch.

Oh, Sam, my darling, please don't be disappointed in me. I couldn't bear it if I weren't all that you want me to be. Her thoughts overcame her and she moaned softly, "Love me, Sam; please love me."

In answer to her request, she felt Sam's long, lean body press against hers. Her body reacted of its own volition. Zevia's lips parted with a cry that echoed the depth of her need. Sam's body, in harmony with hers, led them both to such a tumultuous crest that they were each transported to an indescribable sphere. Sam's voice was hoarse as with spasmodic shudders he repeated over and over, "I love you, Zevia. I love you."

There was a deep, quick silence as Sam held Zevia close in his arms, her head snuggled on his chest.

"Sam?" Zevia questioned softly.

"Yes, my love?" His voice was loving and languid.

"Are you disappointed, after eighty-nine days and twenty-one hours?" she whispered.

Sam raised up on his elbow to look into her lovely face.

"With my own beautiful, starry-eyed Zevia waiting for me? Never could I be disappointed, my love." He kissed her tenderly, her eyelids, her cheeks . . . he searched and found her mouth with his own. He held her as close as he could in a soft, loving embrace.

"You could never disappoint me, my sweet."

Zevia sighed a small sound of contentment. She was

loved. She knew that never again in her lifetime would she want for more than she had at last—the real, true love of an honest, good man.

Twenty-nine

Zevia was not prepared for the swell of emotion that flooded over her when she and Sam stepped from the train in Portland to find her father and grandfather waiting on the platform.

She looked at her father. She could not hold back the gasp that sprang from her mouth. He was still straight and tall, as she had remembered him. Still strong, still clear-eyed, still handsome—however, now his hair was almost totally white. It made the planes of his high cheekbones and the contours of his smooth brown skin appear more deeply etched. Standing beside her father, her grandfather seemed smaller, more stooped, frailer than she remembered. His welcoming smile and the twinkle in his dark eyes, however, meant that he was happy to see her.

Alex Sinclair held his arms open and Zevia ran to him to be folded into his strong embrace.

"Papa!"

"Liebchen!" Alex Sinclair murmured, as he held his daughter close. "You're here at last!"

He looked over his daughter's head, recognized Sam, and reached to shake Sam's hand.

"Thank you for bringing my daughter home safe."

"Oh, I had to do it, sir!" Sam plunged into the real

reason for his presence. "Your daughter and I have been married for almost a month now."

Alex Sinclair looked into his daughter's face, saw her nod affirmatively at her new husband, and saw the happiness in her eyes. He acknowledged the love and pride for his daughter that he saw in Sam's look as he responded to Sam's strong handshake. Here is a good man, Alex thought. My Miffy found a good man.

Sam continued to speak. "I hope you'll accept me, sir, as . . . as your son-in-law."

Alex pumped Sam's hand vigorously and responded with a warm smile.

"Done and done, sir! Welcome home! Come, you must meet Zevia's Opa."

"My pleasure, sir." Sam shook hands with the older man. "Sam Cross, sir," he said.

Zevia's grandfather thumped Sam heartily on the back.

"Zevia couldn't do better. A man of the sea is a man after my heart," he insisted.

Everyone piled into the buggy and headed the few miles out of town to Stoningham and the house on the knoll.

Zevia thought her home had never been more appealing. The long front windows that looked out over the magnificent ocean, her father's studio, filled with tables of blueprints and plans as well as ship models, the everlasting pines that sang with the wind's whispers—she could hardly wait to see it all again.

She could hardly wait to walk around the outside to check for herself the permanence she knew she'd find. She realized suddenly how much she had missed every stone wall, every familiar path. Much had changed in her life. She was not the same Zevia who had left Stoningham, but this house on the knoll had not changed. It was still familiar to her, and it was home.

Some of the neighbors had stopped by to bring food to welcome Zevia home, and also to meet her husband. She had waved goodbye to the last few stragglers, and she watched as the buggies made their way down the hill. Their lanterns bounced in the dark as the clumsy vehicles swayed from side to side. When the last light had disappeared down the road, Zevia went inside to join the menfolk who sat around the fireplace. A cheerful fire burned. It was a welcome sight, Zevia thought.

Sam stood up immediately when he saw Zevia come into the room. He drew a chair close to the fire for her. Maine nights could be mighty cool.

"Your neighbors are sure nice, Zevia," he said. "Remind me a lot of the friendly folk back in Nantucket. Always ready to help."

"Always ready to satisfy their curiosity, you mean," she smiled at him. "They couldn't wait to meet you—see what you were like."

She couldn't sit down just yet. Restlessly, she walked about the room, fingered the quilt on the couch that her grandmother had sewn. A knitted afgan lay on her grandmother's chair as if she had just dropped it there. Zevia could visualize her Oma sitting there, her head ever bowed, her fingers busy with handwork. Zevia felt her eyes fill with tears. She furtively brushed them aside and joined the men. She was grateful that when she took the seat Sam offered her, he did not mention her tears, merely squeezed her hand gently, but she knew he had noticed them.

Sam spoke. "I was telling your father and grandfather that a lot of our trouble was started by Dieter Fleishman."

"The same Dieter Fleishman that was my 'father's' nephew?" Alex asked. "As I remember, the Prussian had little to do with him. Or any of his own family, for that matter. Often wondered if it was because of me, *Schwartze Kind,* black child, they called me."

"Papa, I believe he hated you, was jealous because you got what he thought was rightfully his."

Zevia's grandfather drew in a draft of smoke from his pipe, exhaled before he spoke.

"Well, there was a paper signed by Alex's father and the German. You see, Homer Sinclair could read and write some, same as me. Wasn't many colored could read, but we could, and Homer wouldn't let you go, Alex, until that indenture thing was signed. I remember that. Said that Alex was to get trainin' an' care until he was eighteen as pay for bein' the soldier's servant."

Alex shook his head regretfully.

"Just the same, makes me sick, Zevia, to know that the scoundrel bothered you. He had no right."

"All behind us now, sir. Zevia and I intend to get on with our lives."

"Of course. You're right, Sam. Can't tell you how proud I am of both of you. Seems to me you've been through hell and torment, but you're both stronger for it, I believe."

"I understand, sir, that you have a new ship coming 'down the ways.' "

"Indeed. I hope you and Miffy will be here to see the launching—in about ten days."

"We have two weeks before the *Queen* will be ready to sail," Sam told him. "We'll be here."

Zevia's grandfather stood up and stretched.

"Well, young folks, it's been quite a day. So happy to

have you home again, Zev. I'm off to bed. I'm for an early start come mornin'."

"Opa! You're still fishing?"

"Every day the Lord sends. Can't think of a better thing to do."

Zevia hugged him. " 'Night, Opa. Sleep well."

Sam shook the old man's hand, surprised at the strength he felt in the seventy-year-old man's palm.

"Guess we've all had quite a day," Alex Sinclair said. "I want to make my rounds before I turn in. Sam," he turned to his son-in-law, "you and Miffy have the big room upstairs that faces the ocean. Hope you'll be comfortable there."

"Thank you, sir. We'll be fine," Sam assured him, as he stood with his arm around his wife. She turned to face him.

"Sam, you go on up. I'll be along soon. I'd . . . I'd like to make the rounds with Papa."

"I understand, my love."

"I won't keep her long, Sam, I promise," Alex said.

Zevia found a shawl on a hook in the back hall. She threw it around her shoulders. She knew it was one of her grandmother's, and she could swear she could sense her Oma's presence as she followed her father outside. He carried a lantern that cast dancing shadows as they walked to the barn to check Samson and the cows. This was a nightly ritual, something her father had done as far back as she could remember.

"Must always be sure everything is safe and secure," he'd always say. "Security is the first line of defense."

"Come, *Liebling,* we do our checking."

Zevia linked her arm into her father's. They made their way to the barn, where Samson rumbled a throaty greeting. The cows lay quiet, placidly chewing their cud.

"Fine, as usual, my friend," Alex said to the horse. "You're as handsome as any Lippizaner, you know." He patted the animal and gave him his nightly treat, a bit of carrot from his pocket.

"You know, *Liebling,* Samson would not let me leave the barn without giving him that piece of carrot. I swear he'd follow me into the house if ever I forgot it."

"You've spoiled him, Papa, and you know it."

They made their way to the front of the house. The Atlantic Ocean pounded furiously on the rocky shoreline below the knoll. The undulating waves that rushed forward crashed endlessly, foamed and billowed, and receded only to repeat their salty excursion without ceasing.

"I'm so happy to have you home, Miffy, but I'm sad that your mother and grandmother aren't here to be part of your homecoming."

Zevia was startled. Rarely during her growing up years had her father talked about her mother.

He indicated the rockers on the front porch.

"Can we sit for a moment, *Liebchen?* You're not too chilly?"

"No, Papa, not at all."

He stared out over the dark water.

"You asked me once why your momma died. I told you then that I didn't know. But . . . I know why your momma died. I didn't love her enough."

"Oh, Papa, that's not true!"

"Yes, Miffy, it's true. It was all my fault. I wanted so much to *be* somebody, to prove to everyone that I was a real man, not just an indentured servant, obliged to cater to the whims and caprices of a moody Hessian soldier. So I struggled and worked, day and night, to reach my goal. Adelaide wanted more, she needed more, she demanded more from me than I could give, much as my foster father had. I had to keep something for myself, I *had* to, and God knows, I loved your mother. It wasn't because of you that she died. It was me. I couldn't give her all of me, and that's what she wanted. I've deprived you of a mother's love, and I'll always be sorry about that . . ."

"Papa, don't talk like that. I don't feel deprived. Couldn't miss what I didn't have. And I always had you. You were there. You're my papa, and I love you."

"Well, I do know one thing for sure . . ."

"Yes, Papa?"

"I'm mighty proud of you, that's what! I don't think there's another young woman, colored or white, who's had the grit to do what you did. Some adventure you've had, young lady."

Sudden, clarity struck Zevia. She heard herself say, "I did it because of you, Papa. I never wanted to be a disappointment to you. I wanted you to know how proud I was of my name, Zevia Sinclair."

Her voice almost broke when she remembered the near disaster that had fallen into her innocent life when she was in Boston. It seemed so long ago, as if it had all happened to another person. Indeed, that Zevia was a stranger. It was as if she had never existed.

Her father was speaking.

"I won't keep you from your husband, *Liebchen*. Happiness is all I want for you. Love your captain, trust each other, and believe in the goodness of each other. He's a fine man, your Sam Cross is, but then, you know that, eh, Miffy?" Her father smiled at her in the lantern light.

"Yes, Papa, I know he's a good man."

"Go to him."

Zevia kissed her father on the forehead before she left him. Their brief talk had been a clarifying epiphany for each of them.

"Goodnight, Papa."

"Goodnight, Miffy."

Alex Sinclair sat for a while, rocking his chair gently back and forth. He listened to the plunging waves that assaulted the coastline.

Well, Adelaide, you can rest easy. Zevia is happy. I know you are pleased to hear that. She's just what you wanted, a beautiful, strong-willed, but loving daughter. You'd be proud of her.

When Zevia reached the bedroom, she found Sam waiting for her, standing fully clothed in front of the window, looking out and listening to the ocean.

"Thanks, Sam, for letting me have those moments alone with Papa. We needed that time together."

"I knew how much you wanted a few moments alone. It was important to both of you."

"That's because you understand me, Sam. You scare me, you know me so well."

"Because I love you, Zev."

"Tell me again, Sam. Can't hear it too often."

"Do better than that." He put his arms around her and pulled her close. "Come to bed and I'll show you."

"Aye, Captain," Zevia whispered into his chest. She loved the strong scent of his skin lotion. Her senses were heightened to an unbelievable awareness. They stood silent, listened to the thundering waves on the rocks below. It mirrored their own emotion.

"Do you feel the pull of the ocean, Zevia?" Sam asked.

"Yes, Sam, it has a presence like no other force. Like something you can't escape. It calls you."

"It's like we said before. The ocean is strong, it's purifying, and when it comes into shore, it wipes the beach clean, taking all debris and misery with it."

"I know one thing, Sam Cross," Zevia said lightly, "it's not going to take you anywhere without me, your wife, Zevia Sinclair Cross. You can be sure of that."

She raised her face to his, and as his mouth covered hers, she responded with soft murmurs of her own. She'd always hunger for Sam's love, his tender touch.

Their mouths clung and soon her fingers were busily unbuttoning his shirt while he worked on the buttons of her blouse. Frantic in their eagerness for contact with each other, they struggled to rid their bodies of their restrictive clothing.

Zevia moaned as her husband, his magnificent bronze body reflected in the light of the lamp, excited her. At last, this man that she loved was hers and hers alone.

Sam moved his strong, lean fingers over her naked body, loving her with every adoring touch. His mouth sought her lips, her cheeks, her neck. He nibbled at her ears as Zevia trembled in anticipation. Her skin was aflame as her husband's knowing caresses ministered to her hungry body.

No ship rocked beneath their feet, yet both lovers knew a breathless lift that summoned them to a higher plane.

"Oh, Sam," Zevia whimpered, "love me, love me now."

Sam buried his face in the valley between her lovely breasts and carried her to their bed. Zevia tightened her arms around her husband's neck and offered herself to the man she loved. Tears of fulfillment flooded her eyes as she realized the depth of her love for the man in her arms.

The fire that had kindled between them burned as bright as the radiance of forever. The trauma of the past was forgotten, and each of them reveled in the glory of the moment. Sam's slender fingers moved lightly over Zevia's soft skin like the touch of an angel's wing. Zevia responded with faltering whimpers as Sam's touch took away her breath.

The ocean outside their windows echoed the tumultuous throbbing of their hearts. The pounding sounds were amplified in Sam's ears as he tried to moderate his excitement to keep pace with the stirring passion of Zevia, his beloved.

Suddenly, an exquisite convulsion shook him, his head was thrown back, and his movement was confirmed by Zevia's now inflamed body. She shuddered all over as her own needs were met as she welcomed him home.

A new moon traced a silvery path across the shimmering water and into the room where the lovers lay. The haunting cry of a loon sounded as it flew across the face of the moon. It disturbed Zevia and she moved restlessly in her husband's arms.

Instinctively, Sam tightened his arm around her and drew her close.

"You're home safe, my love. Sleep," he said. He kissed

her cheek gently as she settled into his arms. "You'll always be safe with me, my love."

Epilogue

The *Darling,* as the Worrells decided to name her, was launched from their own boatyard in Portland. Both brothers were present, as was their nephew, Austin Talbot, who greeted Sam and Zevia warmly. He responded graciously when Sam introduced him to Zevia's father.

"Delighted to meet you, Mr. Sinclair. Heard so much about you, and I must say, the *Darling* is a magnificent ship."

"Thank you for your kind words," Alex answered with a formal bow. "Now, if she'll just go down the ways properly . . ."

"Don't fret, Papa," Zevia reassured him. "She will."

"I'm sure she'll do just fine," Sam added. "Have every confidence."

Zevia thought her husband looked very handsome. As a new Worrell captain, he wore a white captain's uniform. His hair curled softly beneath his cap, and his tall, straight figure was outlined by the blinding white clothing, which only enhanced his bronze, sun-kissed skin. Oh God, she prayed silently, take care of us and our love for each other.

Zevia wore a navy-blue wool suit. A sheer cream-colored blouse with ruffles at the throat framed her face.

She wore a navy bonnet trimmed with white grosgrain ribbon around the brim.

Sam's heart rejoiced when he saw his wife come to stand beside him. He tucked her hand under his elbow. His happiness knew no bounds as he noted her beautifully serene composure.

"You look lovely," he whispered to her.

"Thank you, Sam." Zevia smiled at him and pressed her hand gently on his arm in response.

The *Darling* sat majestically on the cradle. Hundreds of wedges had been placed under her the day before. When the tide was ready, the blocks would be knocked out and the ship would slide down the greased cradle or "standing ways" to the ocean.

Sam explained it to his wife.

"When a ship is being built, honey, she rests on keel and bilge blocks. When she's about to be launched, she's held by a cradle. She'll only move at the proper time. In hot weather, she can't rest too long on the ways because her weight could squeeze out the grease under her and she can't start to move."

"Why is she launched stern end first, Sam?"

"Oh, Zev, the stern is the most fragile end of the ship, and when the vessel enters the water, the ship could be damaged if the stern fails to lift. That's why most ships are launched stern first."

"It's so exciting, Sam."

"It is. You know," he looked at the excited crowd of people at the dockside, "I think every able-bodied person from Portland is down here this morning. I wonder how many of them know your father designed this ship."

"Daresay, not many. Papa and the Worrells keep most of their business practices close."

"Just as well, probably wouldn't believe that a colored man could do such a thing. But," he added, "if deep in your heart you know what you can do, who you are, and what you want out of life, why not go after it?" He smiled at her sober face. "Am I right, Zev, or am I right?" he teased.

"You're right, husband mine. You're right."

And that's the way it should be, Zevia thought. Know who you are and what you want from life. This crowd of people are all here at this spot today because of one man, my papa, an indentured servant who challenged life. How could I ever do less? she wondered.

She looked at the man who stood beside her. He had come into her life, had comforted her, taught her, worried about her, championed her, loved her. She had traveled many paths to find him, but now the search was over. As long as Sam loved her, Zevia knew that together they could conquer anything. They already had life's sweetest gift—love.

FOR THE VERY BEST IN ROMANCE—
DENISE LITTLE PRESENTS!

AMBER, SING SOFTLY (0038, $4.99)
by Joan Elliott Pickart

Astonished to find a wounded gun-slinger on her doorstep, Amber Prescott can't decide whether to take him in or put him out of his misery. Since this lonely frontierswoman can't deny her longing to have a man of her own, who nurses him back to health, while savoring the glorious possibilities of the situation. But what Amber doesn't realize is that this strong, handsome man is full of surprises!

A DEEPER MAGIC (0039, $4.99)
by Jillian Hunter

From the moment wealthy Margaret Rose and struggling physician Ian MacNeill meet, they are swept away in an adventure that takes them from the haunted land of Aberdeen to a primitive, faraway island—and into a world of danger and irresistible desire. Amid the clash of ancient magic and new science Margaret and Ian find themselves falling helplessly in love.

SWEET AMY JANE (0050, $4.99)
by Anna Eberhardt

Her horoscope warned her she'd be dealing with the wrong sort of man. And private eye Amy Jane Chadwick was used to dealing with the wrong kind of man, due to her profession. But nothing prepared her for the gorgeously handsome Max, a former professional athlete who is being stalked by an obsessive fan. And from the moment they meet, sparks fly and danger follows!

MORE THAN MAGIC (0049, $4.99)
by Olga Bicos

This classic romance is a thrilling tale of two adventurers who set out for the wilds of the Arizona territory in the year 1878. Seeking treasure, an archaeologist and an astronomer find the greatest prize of all—love.